Hristina E

CW01642871

Fire

Book 1

Ash

Fire. Book 1. Ash

London, 2025

hrisisart@gmail.com

Instagram: @hristinabloomfield

www.authorhristinabloomfield.com

-Chapter One-

The Burning Town

It was a hot, sunny day. One of those days when the heat engulfs you, and you start to sweat the moment you step outside. Cassy was walking with her nephews near the mountain. On one side of the Mountain Path, the forest began, and there were tall trees and bushes. On the other side of the path was the river. This was the only way to get to her sister-in-law's house with even a slight air of coolness. Normally, greenery surrounded the path, but now some of the bushes had sprouted, and others were withered. Dry, yellowed leaves covered the ground beside them. In the spring, the mountain water fountains flowed, and people poured clean, cold water from them, but now, after the month-long August heat, they had dried up. The small waterfalls that used to flow in spring were now also dry. Everything around seemed to have died down. The heat had driven the animals and insects to hiding places.

Cassy walked slowly and talked to the twins, Rita and Bobo. The children asked her thousands of questions, and she found it difficult to answer them all at once. Since Eleonora's husband had disappeared, she had been helping her sister-in-law raise the two kids. Eleonora was the mayor of the town, and also the sister of Steve, Cassy's second husband. She was also the reason that Steve and she had moved to Balkan. The town was small, the people were friendly, and only in rare exceptions did something bad happen.

Cassy had been the chief of police in Balkan for four years. Before they moved, she had worked in the Intelligence Agency in the capital. After her partner, Billy, suddenly died, she had fallen into depression, and as a result, her marriage to Steve had begun to slowly disintegrate. Then Eleonora had offered Cassy a job, and the family decided to move to the smaller town.

As she walked, Cassy occasionally wiped the sweat that ran down her neck. Her long, curly brown hair was tied in a ponytail that almost reached her waist. The twins' hair was also curly, and often, people in town thought that she and Eleonora were related by blood. The two women looked very much alike. Steve, however, was different. He had inherited his mother's blonde hair, and his eyes were mottled green.

Cassy walked behind the children, trying to avoid the nettles that grew on one side of the path. The twins' questions had stopped. The long journey from the police station and the heat had tired them, and they walked in silence. They all tried to hide from the sun by walking single file in the shadow of the mountain. It usually took them thirty minutes to walk from the town centre to Eleonora's house, but today their journey took longer. After several rests, they finally arrived at the large, beautiful house where her sister-in-law and her family lived. The nanny took the twins, and Cassy walked back to the police station. This time, she decided to go via the main town road. She was thirsty, and her water bottle was empty. She had to stop by the nearest store and buy a new one.

As she crossed the bridge connecting the trail to the town's main road, Cassy received a message from Steve. He had left for a few days to visit his mother, and let her know he had arrived safely. Steve had been visiting his mother more and more lately, and Cassy wondered if she was the reason. Their marriage had been stagnant for a long time. They thought that moving here would renew their relationship, that the change would bring in something exciting and new, but that had never happened. They had been living together more like roommates than husband and wife for a long time now. They rarely talked and no longer made plans to go anywhere together unless they had to.

Their marriage had died, but they continued to live together, as if by habit. There were a few things that bound them. The one good thing they both took care of with pleasure, and both loved very much, was their dog, Charlie. Dear Charlie, he had been small and defenceless when they had found him on the street. But now he had become the most pampered dog in town. Cassy smiled at the thought of him.

She crossed the bridge and headed for the small grocery store near the river. She had almost reached the front door when a loud crash interrupted her thoughts. Cassy looked ahead and saw a puff of smoke in the distance. Something had probably caught fire. Fires were not uncommon in the area in the dry, hot weather. *Let's hope the fire doesn't grow*, Cassy thought, and she decided not to go to the store. Instead, she kept walking, worried by the growing ball of smoke that was drifting over the city. Then she realized that the smoke was coming from the centre of the town, and she started running. Slowly at first, but after seeing other people running in panic, she started running as fast as she could.

The sound of sirens stopped her. Her colleagues had been activated. Something was happening, but Cassy was far away and couldn't see what. She was about to take her work phone from her back pocket but remembered that she had left it in the office. Her personal phone was on her, but she didn't have her colleagues' phone numbers in her personal phone, in an effort to keep her professional life separate from her personal life. *Big mistake*, she told herself. Then she stopped and looked around, trying to figure out where the danger was coming from. She looked at the ball of smoke again and decided to go towards it. Cassy headed for the riverbed, hoping to get a better view from there. However, the trees on the embankment prevented her from seeing exactly what was burning in the distance, so she tried to climb a linden tree. She had almost climbed it when she felt a vibration, followed by a loud explosion, which knocked her to the ground. Cassy got up slowly and looked in the direction the explosion had come from. She saw that flames had engulfed one of the old warehouses near the block where she and Steve lived. She tried to see what was going on, but she was still far away. The block was probably on fire too, she thought, and her heart sank with worry. Her dog was inside; she had to go and get him out of the apartment.

Cassy started running again. The heat grew stronger; panicked people ran in different directions and often bumped into her. She realized she was the only one running toward the fire, while everyone else was trying to escape from it. Just as she reached the bridge she had to cross to get to her flat, she heard another explosion. More smoke and flames engulfed the surrounding buildings, and the old wooden bridge that Cassy had planned to cross sheared off on one side and fell into the riverbed with a big crash. Several people fell from it. She stopped and stared at them. She was relieved to see that, miraculously, all the people successfully floated out of the river.

Cassy was startled at first by what had happened, then looked ahead and continued running down the sidewalk toward the next bridge. It was stable, made of strong iron and concrete. The chance of this bridge falling quickly was minimal, at least in her opinion. She was trying to make her way through the crowd that was fleeing the flames. However, people pushed her back and prevented her from moving. Instead of moving forward, she seemed to be going backwards. After several attempts to push through the crowd, Cassy stopped, looked around, and wondered what she could do to get to the flat faster.

The road was full of cars, and more and more panic-stricken people were coming from both sidewalks. She looked around once more and walked down the road, trying to avoid the cars coming her way. Some of the drivers cursed at her; others told her she was crazy and that she should stop walking towards the fire. However, she did not pay attention to them. She passed them and looked at the burning buildings on the other side of the river. Soon, the cars stopped, and she was able to reach the bridge, which was also crowded with people running towards her. Cassy tried to make her way through the crowd, but each time, people dragged her with them and pushed her back. Finally, the crowd thinned out, and she was relieved to see that now she would be able to cross the bridge, albeit slowly.

She had just crossed the bridge and headed towards the building where they lived when another explosion echoed through the air. This time, the explosion came from the other part of the town. Screaming people and sirens deafened the village. It was as if everyone had been in hell for just a few minutes. Black smoke clouds filled the air, and it was hard for everyone to breathe.

Cassy looked around; her building, the one her dog Charlie was in, had started to burn on one side. She ran towards it, trying to ignore the heat. Just before she entered the block, she heard her name. Someone was calling her. Cassy turned to see her neighbour's flushed face.

'Cassy!' said Marina. 'Don't go in there. There is no one on the block. Everyone left on time.'

'I have to get Charlie,' Cassy said and turned her back on Marina, walking towards the front door of the building.

'Steve took Charlie out a few minutes ago. He's not there,' her neighbour said, reaching out to grab Cassy's arm and stop her from entering the burning building.

'No, Steve can't have taken him. He is with his mother.'

'I swear, I saw him with my own eyes going out with Charlie,' cried Marina.

Cassy shook her head in disbelief, opened the front door, and stepped into the smoky lobby. She looked around but could see nothing through the smoke. Her eyes began to water, and her breathing became laboured. She began to feel in front of her, finally felt the warm banister of the stairs and began to slowly climb up. When she reached the first floor, Cassy saw an open window and went over to catch her breath. The smoke on the floor was still not too thick, so she continued to the second floor. As she moved up slowly, she felt the flames coming from the south side of the block. There was still no sign of fire on the north side where their flat was, and that gave her hope to continue. Then she would think about how she was going to get out of here; now, the most important thing was to get to Charlie.

As she climbed the last few steps, Cassy wondered why she didn't hear a dog barking; if her dog was fine, he would be barking. With even greater alarm, she approached the flat and saw that the front door was open. The flat wasn't on fire. She made her way inside and quickly walked around the small space. Charlie wasn't there. *But where is he then?* she wondered. If someone had opened the door, Charlie would most likely have gone out into the street. This thought first calmed her, then worried her. Her dog was now outside, and she didn't know where he was or if she would be able to save him.

Cassy left the apartment with a damp towel over her face, then she began to slowly descend the stairs to the lower floor. The smoke was getting thicker, and with each step, it became more difficult for her to breathe. In the end, she could see almost nothing, as her eyes were watering, so she went by intuition. From the south side of the block, there was a loud noise, and something collapsed. Cassy became worried and walked down the stairs in a panic, falling, then getting up quickly. Finally, she found the front door and went out. When she got outside and looked around, she saw only burning buildings. There weren't any people at all. There were no screams or cries, instead there was the terrible noise of burning. Around her, there were many sliding doors, windows, and other objects that blocked her view.

Cassy walked towards the bridge, hoping to cross it, but the abandoned cars on it were already on fire, and the chance of one of them exploding was high. She looked around again, and panic filled her. She was trapped. She couldn't go down into the river; the dam was too high, and the river was black now, full of debris from the burning buildings. Asphalt, melted by the heat, was sliding towards the river. Her only escape was to go to the mountain. However, her way there was blocked by flames and burning debris as well. The asphalt on the street she had to cross to get to the other side had also melted and turned into a thick black liquid in places. Cassy looked down at her shoes. The good news was that she hadn't changed her clothes and had stuck with her sturdy police shoes rather than trainers. The bad news was that they too could get stuck and sink into the melting asphalt. However, Cassy decided to take a chance. She looked back at the street in front of her and quickly ran to the opposite sidewalk. *So far, so good*, she told herself. She looked down the next street to assess the risk. She had to move; the sooner she got out of here, the better. To avoid the sticky asphalt, she had to step only on concrete and stones. Cassy carefully hopped from place to place. She had to walk past three burning houses and prayed that none of them would fall on her. Luckily for her, she passed without a problem.

However, the heat began to overwhelm her. Even though she was already close to the Mountain Path, Cassy could feel her strength starting to leave her, and she could barely move. The air around her trembled with heat, and she felt as if she had indeed found herself in hell. Her breathing quickened, her body was drenched in sweat, her hair stuck to her, and her legs and arms were beginning to swell. The smoke thickened even more, and Cassy slowly began to surrender and slide to the ground. She leaned against one of the buildings and tried to muster the strength to continue. The air was so hot that every breath she took through the now-dry towel caused her intense pain. She could feel the hot air entering first her nostrils, continuing its way through her throat, and slowly descending to her lungs. The pain of inhaling was so strong that it made her cough violently.

This is the end, she thought as she tried to catch her breath; *this must be the end of my life*. Tears welled up in her eyes; she could feel them making their way down her cheeks. Cassy tried to wipe them away but failed. She didn't have the strength to raise her hand, and the towel slowly fell to her feet. At that moment, she felt someone douse her with water. The water wasn't cold; it was lukewarm, but it felt refreshing to Cassy.

'Put this towel in front of your nose, and keep breathing through it,' said a male voice. Cassy did as she was told. The man grabbed her by the waist and made her stand up.

'Gather some more strength,' he said. 'A few more steps, and we will be at the stream.'

Cassy had to go. Her legs hurt, but at least her breathing was easier. The man held her for a while, then made her stop, picked her up in his arms, and began to carry her. Cassy could feel him running and wondered how anyone could do that in this heat.

'Here, we have arrived,' said the man, and he let her feet touch the ground. Cassy stood for a short time and then sat down on the ground. She looked around as far as she could and saw that they were at the Old Stream. The stream had shrunk, so the water that flowed down it was not deep, but it was cold. The man began to collect some of it and pour it over Cassy's face. She felt better from the coolness the water gave her.

'Don't drink; just wet your mouth,' he advised her.

Cassy nodded and began scooping the mountain water into her palms and splashing it over her face.

'Do you feel better?' he asked.

'Yes,' she answered hoarsely. The warm air still hurt her with each inhalation and exhalation.

'We have to climb up. Rest for a few minutes, then we will have to continue.'

She nodded and stared at the man in front of her. He was dressed in a fireman's uniform, and his face was blackened by the smoke, but his eyes sparkled. Cassy knew this man. Burke was the fire chief. He, like her, had moved from the big city. Two years ago, after Eleonora's husband disappeared without a trace, Burke had taken his place. Cassy had seen him at several community meetings but had hardly spoken to him. Her first impression of him was that he was a man of action. He was not one of those people who grumbled about bureaucracy; he took his duties seriously and professionally. Cassy now thought that her judgment of Burke had been correct and that she owed him her life.

'Thanks!' she said, trying to get up.

'Rest another minute. We still have a little time. The buildings near us are not about to collapse yet.'

Cassy nodded and dropped to the ground. Her thoughts turned to Steve. Did he find out about the fire? And what happened to Charlie? She hoped one of her neighbours had carried him out of the building and taken him with them.

'We have to go,' Burke said and helped her up. They began to climb slowly. The thick trees and bushes made it difficult for them to move. Cassy grabbed onto the branches to help herself up, but soon, her already injured hands from the heat began to bleed and ache with every touch.

'Take off your T-shirt,' Burke told her. Cassy took a step back and looked at him worriedly.

'Take it off!' he insisted and stepped towards her. She got scared and took another step back.

'We need to cover your palms with it,' he explained.

This time, she listened. She undressed and handed him the blackened T-shirt. Burke tore it into several pieces, motioned for Cassy to approach him, and wrapped the cloth tightly around her palms.

'I didn't know you were so sensitive,' he told her.

'Usually I'm not, but the circumstances are a bit unusual.'

'Yes,' Burke said, gesturing for her to move on. He had also benefitted from the water in the stream, and now Cassy could see his face. Burke wasn't scared, she found, but he was very thoughtful the whole time they were climbing up. They both grabbed roots and branches, and with their help, climbed up to one of the cliffs overlooking the city. The moment they got onto a ledge, they lay down to catch their breath and rest.

-Chapter Two-

Soot and Ash

Cassy sat on the hard rock looking down. It was getting dark, but she could still see the billows of black smoke rising from the burning city. After taking a few breaths, she sat up next to Burke. The man was silent and also watched what was happening below. Now and then, they could hear cracks as a window or balcony fell from a building, but in general, the city began to smoulder, and the fire weakened.

Cassy stared at Burke. He seemed to be weighing and considering something.

'What's wrong?' she asked him.

'Why do you think something is bothering me?'

'Your face suggests it. I'm a police inspector. I've learned to figure people out.'

Burke turned to her and looked into her eyes, but he didn't answer her question. Instead, he got up and began to examine the rock. Then his gaze returned to her.

'Perhaps you should turn that judgment on yourself,' he finally said. 'Why didn't you leave the town?'

'I was trying to save my dog,' she admitted.

'Did you save him?'

'No. I went into the flat, but Charlie wasn't there. A neighbour probably took him because the front door was left open.'

Burke nodded. His gaze returned to the town.

'Why were you still there?' Cassy asked.

'It's my job. I saw you leave the building, but I was far away. It took me a while to find you.'

'Thanks for saving my life,' Cassy said and then coughed. It was still difficult for her to speak. Her legs hurt. She had a strong urge to take off her shoes, but she knew that if she did, she wouldn't be able to put them back on.

'The Small Stream is nearby,' Burke said, breaking the silence. 'We can go and freshen up in a little while.'

'Okay,' Cassy agreed, and like him, she looked at the smoking city. Part of the town was engulfed in soot and ash. Another part was still burning. In some places only, embers seemed to remain. As twilight fell, Cassy could see the flames burning brighter and brighter within. Whatever had caused all this was something no one could quickly deal with.

'What do you think caused this fire?' Cassy asked.

'Fires,' said Burke.

'What?' She did not understand.

'It's not one fire. I think the city was set on fire, with six separate fires,' said Burke, still watching the burning town, then he turned to her.

'What? How so? And why do you think there are six?' Cassy's breath stopped at what she heard. She asked the questions quickly and then coughed from the effort of speaking.

'Calm down and breathe slowly and deeply. Keep putting something in front of your mouth and nose because even though you can't see them, the soot and ashes are in the atmosphere even here.'

Burke pulled a pack of wet wipes from his pocket, unfolded one of them, placed it in front of his mouth and nose, and inhaled and exhaled several times deeply. Then he showed the wet wipe to Cassy. The wipe was blackened on the front.

'You have to be careful what you inhale,' he said.

Cassy took a part of her torn T-shirt and started breathing through it.

'Why six fires?' she asked him after a while.

'Let's go up to the other rock, and I'll show you,' Burke said and helped her up. They began to climb up. This time, they were walking along one of the mountain paths, and it was easier for them to move. When they reached the next stream, they stayed there for a short time to refresh themselves, then continued to climb. It was already after midnight when they reached the Sharp Stone, as the locals called the rock.

Burke and Cassy sat down on the cool rock and looked out at the smouldering town again. In places, the town could not be seen, probably because of the smoke and soot that hung in the air. Burke was right. From up high, Cassy could see the damage more clearly, and to her surprise, she found that the fire had affected only the central part of the town. There was no sign of flames in the lower or upper part. The forest hadn't started burning either. It was as if someone had assessed the risk and had set the town on fire so that it would not engulf everything around it. Cassy looked over at Burke, but it was dark, and she couldn't see his face well.

'Weird, right?' she said.

'What's weird?' Burke asked, turning to her.

'Only the central part is burned, but you already know that, don't you?'

'Yes. I believe this was a controlled fire.'

'Do you think someone did it on purpose?'

'I'm convinced. But before I go down and look, I can't say either who or how.'

Cassy sat back on the cool stone and sighed heavily. She was very tired. She was also hungry and thirsty, and the tension made her want to scream. Why would anyone want to set fire to the city? There weren't many criminals in this town, and there weren't many feuds. According to her, it was one of the most peaceful cities in the country. Of course, her job brought her into contact with all kinds of people, but this was different. From what she could see, whoever had done this, if Burke was right, had to be someone with a lot of hatred in his heart.

Cassy stood up and looked down again. 'Why six?' she asked.

Burke got up, came over, and sat next to her. 'Count the smouldering buildings,' he said.

She counted them. There were two on the left, two on the right, and two in the middle of the damaged city.

'You're right – there are six.'

'I think there are six abandoned buildings. Whoever set the town on fire gave enough time for people to evacuate before the flames engulfed their houses.'

Cassy didn't agree with that but decided not to argue.

'But who would do such a thing?' she wondered. 'Who would harbour so much anger?'

Burke didn't answer, but something told her he had a suspect. She was just about to ask him something else, but he got up and walked away.

'It's a good idea to sleep. It will be a long time before we can go down to the town again.'

'Okay,' Cassy agreed, looking down at the smouldering remains of the downtown area, then lay down and curled up, hoping to fall asleep quickly. Something told her that Burke would stay awake. She stared at him, then closed her eyes and thought that she herself would not calm down until she knew what had happened to her relatives and her dog. She only now remembered that Eleonora was also in the centre of the city. Cassy hoped her sister-in-law had left it in time. Thus, carried away in her thoughts from one thing to another, she at last fell asleep.

-Chapter Three-

A Ghost Town

The light from the rising sun woke Cassy. She looked around and wondered where she was. The moment she took a breath and smelled the smoke; she remembered the fire. She turned to look at Burke. He was asleep with his back to her, snoring loudly. Cassy rose slowly, her whole body aching. Her arms and legs were covered in sores, some of them inflamed and throbbing. She thought she had to go down to the surviving part of town and find a first-aid kit and painkillers. Then she looked back at the smouldering city. It would be easier and faster to go to the upper part of the town. The cliff they were on was a little off that part, but Cassy thought they could get down quickly. She sighed heavily, and her sigh woke Burke up. He turned and blinked a few times as if realizing where he was, and then he slowly got up. He, like Cassy, looked at the city. Then he heard her moan and looked at her hands and feet.

'You need medical help,' he told her. 'Your burns and wounds will be very painful and will become even more inflamed if we do not wash and disinfect them.'

'I know,' she said. 'Do you think we'll be able to get down to the upper part of the city?'

'We definitely can. I know a direct path. When you're ready, we'll go.'

'I'm ready,' Cassy said and slowly got to her feet. When she looked down, she saw that her ankles were swollen. Some of the skin on them had been burned away and had been replaced with large welts. The sight was horrifying, and she quickly looked away from the wounds. Burke was also up and motioned to her in the direction they should go.

Despite it being early in the day, the August heat was already strong, and the moment they entered the wooded part of the route, the air became even more stuffy. Cassy and Burke could barely catch their breath, but they kept walking. They crossed two small streams, but both were dry. The only thing they could find that somewhat satiated their hunger was a type of wood sorrel that the natives often picked and used in their soups. Burke plucked a few leaves from the sorrel and handed them to Cassy, advising her to chew them slowly. After a while, they found themselves on another rock, from which they were able to view the upper part of the town. Nothing seemed to have been harmed there, but it looked desolate from the lack of people and animals.

Cassy and Burke continued their descent down the mountain for about an hour. When they reached the Mountain Path, as the locals called it, they sat down to rest. Everything around was covered in soot and ash. The air was dirty, but the visibility was better than the night before.

'Where are we going?' she asked.

'We will enter the first house we reach. You need medicine and rest,' said Burke. 'If we find what we need there, I'll let you rest, and I'll try to contact someone in the Rhodopes and tell them that we're here and we're alive.'

Cassy breathed a sigh of relief. Her whole body ached, but she tried to hide her pain from Burke, so as not to bother him.

'The satellite phone transmitters are dead, and I'm unlikely to get range, but I can try the radios,' said Burke.

'There is one in the Sports Base.'

'I'll go there. Are you ready?' he asked her.

Cassy nodded and tried to get up, but her legs wouldn't hold her. Burke stared at her, then approached her and gestured that he would pick her up. She nodded and let him carry her. The houses were not far, but Burke had to put her down several times to rest. At last, they approached a house whose garden gate had been left open. Burke helped Cassy into the garden and let her sit on one of benches. Then he tried to open the front door, but when he couldn't, he went back and broke down the back door. Then he returned to Cassy to get her and carried her into the house. Once inside, Burke placed her on the living room sofa and began searching for medicine, opening every possible cupboard. Cassy tried to hold on, but the pain in her body was becoming unbearable, and she began to moan more and more. Finally, she lay her head on the sofa, gritted her teeth, and began to cry. She hadn't cried like that since she was a child. The pain from her burned and injured body was so intense that she finally started to howl. She curled up on the sofa and tried to wrap her injured arms with the blanket that was left there. During this time, Burke walked around the house and cursed at the occupants.

'There is not even paracetamol here. I'll go to the next house. I hope I find something there,' he said and quickly went outside.

Cassy curled up again and forced herself to ignore the pain. She stared at one of the plants in the room and began to count its leaves. She sometimes used this technique when she was angry or under a lot of pressure. She counted something over and over until she calmed down. This time, it didn't help for long. Pain took over her body again, and tears fell from her eyes. She decided to try counting again when Burke entered the room. He was holding some pills and ointment.

'Okay, one by one,' he said as if to himself. Then he looked around, saw a cup with some liquid in it, picked it up, and sniffed the contents inside.

'Tea,' he said, handing Cassy two pills. 'Take them. It will ease your pain.'

After making sure she had taken the pills, Burke had her lie down. He looked around as if looking for something in particular, and when he didn't find it, he left the room for a while and came back with a man's T-shirt.

'Get dressed,' he said, then he untied one of her shoes and tried to pull it off her foot. Cassy cried out in pain, and Burke gave up for a moment. Then he got up, and she heard him opening and closing the kitchen cupboards. Finally, he returned with a large pair of scissors in his hands. He carefully lifted her right foot and began to slowly cut the top of her shoe with the scissors until he had almost cut it in half. He lowered it slowly to the floor and then did the same with the other shoe. Burke then thoroughly examined her legs, then her arms, and finished with her face.

'Okay,' he finally said. 'I found an anti-inflammatory cream, but it's not enough. It will only be for some of your injuries, so I'll put it where it's most needed. When I apply the cream, it will hurt.'

Cassy stared at him, then nodded. Burke began applying the cream first to her ankles, then to her hands and face. She had her eyes closed and was trying not to scream out in pain.

'Ready. Now we will wait a few minutes for the painkillers to start working. Then I'll help you get up, and we'll both go to the Sports Centre.'

Cassy tried to protest, but Burke stopped her. 'I won't leave you here alone. If you were me, you would do the same.'

She nodded and sat back wearily on the sofa. She didn't have the strength to argue, and she knew from the man's insistent look that he wasn't going to change his mind. Burke got up again and began to search the house for something. Cassy could hear him opening the fridge and cupboards. Finally, he returned with two sandwiches.

'One sandwich for you and one for me. I don't know who lives here, but there is neither medicine nor enough food.'

Cassy rose slightly to eat as much as she could of the sandwich Burke had thoughtfully cut into small bites. She hadn't realized it, but her lips and gums were swollen, and chewing was difficult. She still managed to swallow a quarter of the sandwich.

'Do you feel better?' Burke asked.

'Yes.'

'It's time to go. Will you make it?'

'I will do my best,' she said and got up with difficulty from the sofa.

'I found men's slippers. I think you'd better go with them.'

Cassy put on the slippers and slowly made her way to the front door. As she moved, she could feel Burke's gaze on her back. He followed her, opened the door for her, then grabbed her around the waist and helped her walk faster.

The Sports Centre was located almost at the edge of the town. Two decades ago, the townspeople decided to build a tennis court and pool to use during the warmer months. Residents from the surrounding area collected money and built the Sports Centre. The pool had fallen into disrepair over time because it required a lot of money and care to maintain, while the rest of the facilities had remained. Later, it had been expanded to include a small football field. Cassy often took her nephews there and knew exactly where the first-aid kit was, since she sometimes helped with the children's wounds. Now, as she moved slowly, supported by Burke, she thought that she would never have guessed that someday she would want to enter this building so badly.

The two walked slowly and looked around the abandoned city. The streets were deserted, and ash covered every part of the town. As they walked, some of the ashes that covered the street rose, and if they turned back, they would see the tracks of their steps. Worst of all was the silence. Cassy had never experienced anything like this. It was like she was a character in a horror movie, and she seemed to expect some skeleton or ghost to appear from somewhere at any moment. She looked at Burke. He was also looking around, looking confused, as if he couldn't figure out exactly where he was.

'It's terrible, isn't it?' said Cassy.

Burke stopped, looked at her, and nodded. 'It's like we're in a ghost town,' he said.

They continued to walk until the pain returned. Cassy saw a bench, tried to clear it somewhat of soot, and sat down.

'We are not far,' she said, 'but I need some rest.'

Burke nodded and began to look around as if trying to figure out where he was. Something told Cassy that he knew exactly where he was, and his wonderment was about something else, but she didn't ask. She would do it later. Now she had neither the energy nor the time to think about it. Cassy remained on the bench a little longer, then got up and, supported by Burke, continued to walk down the middle of the street.

When they arrived at the Sports Centre, they found all the doors open and the medicine cabinet broken. The medicine bag was missing. Burke cursed and looked worriedly at Cassy.

'I hope at least the radio works,' he muttered and headed towards one of the open doors. Cassy followed him with a look. She had noticed his tiredness, but as he moved, she also noticed his limp. Burke must have been hurt in some way too, but he hadn't told her. His hands, like hers, looked wounded, and he was most likely in pain.

'The radio station is here, but it's not working,' he called from the other room.

'I guess the battery is dead. Take it out and rub it on a cloth for a while to re-energize it.'

'On what fabric?' Burke asked.

'I did it on my jeans. Come here, I'll show you,' Cassy said.

Burke returned to her with the battery in hand. Cassy reached up and, despite the pain in her hand, picked up the battery and began rubbing it quickly on the fabric of her trousers.

'Rub like this for about a minute. Hopefully that will be enough for a short conversation.'

Burke nodded; he took the battery from her and began rubbing on the fabric of his trousers. While doing it, he looked around. 'Do you think there is anyone else around who needs help?'

'It's possible. Or maybe someone took advantage of the commotion and took the first-aid kit because of the medicine inside.'

'Yes. You're right,' said Burke and went into the other room again. After a while, Cassy heard him trying to talk to someone on the radio. Then she heard him swear again.

'I only managed to say who I was,' he said.

'It might be enough. They'll all want to go back to town soon anyway,' she tried to reassure him.

'It will take at least another twelve hours to assess the risk. You don't have that much time, Cassy. You need more medicine as soon as possible.'

'You need it too, don't you?'

'Yes.'

'Then look in the houses around. I am the chief of police, and I give you permission.' She smiled slightly.

'I wonder how you find the strength to smile,' said Burke, shaking his head sadly and walking out into the street.

Cassy lay down on the small sofa in the room Burke had left her in and tried to breathe calmly. Her breathing was painful, though. The hot air she had taken in yesterday had partially burned her respiratory system, and every breath caused her pain. She looked down at her hands; the blisters had swelled even more. The healing cream Burke had put on them wasn't enough. She needed stronger drugs. *Hopefully, Burke will find something*, she thought, and leaned her head back. She thought about Charlie. Did he survive? She had become very attached to this dog and his strange character. Cassy's parents had told her that she was obsessed with him, and they were probably right. They weren't the type of people who would get a pet. And even better for the animal not to be in their home. Cassy loved her parents, but they never understood her. For them, she should have found a husband, given birth to several children, and stayed at home to take care of the household. For her, this meant her life being controlled by her husband. She preferred to be independent. Yes, she wanted to have children, but not to stay at home all day; that would kill her, little by little.

The sound of a door opening interrupted her thoughts. Burke returned with a paper bag full of medicine. He gave her a nervous smile and poured everything onto the table in front of her.

'I entered three houses and left a note for the owners, to let them know that I was there and to contact me. I found a lot of remedies, but I don't know what most of them are for. We will look into them to see if they would work for us. For starters, we have a pack of painkillers and a full pack of cream for our wounds. We will have enough for one day.'

Burke got up from the chair he was sitting on and walked around the Sports Centre once more. He returned with two half-full bottles of water and a bar of chocolate that had melted from the heat. He poured water into two plastic cups, handed Cassy two pills, and made her take them. He also took two. Then he sat down in the chair and began to take off his fireman's uniform.

'I hope my nakedness doesn't bother you,' he said, looking nervously at her. 'We need to look at my wounds. I can see the front, but for the back, you'll have to help me and, if necessary, smear them with cream.'

Cassy nodded. Burke was burned around his neck, his hands were lacerated, and his ankles were swollen. He kicked off his shoes with a groan, and she noticed that his left leg was starting to turn blue.

'A brick from a building fell on my foot. I didn't think it was serious until this morning.'

'It looks bad,' Cassy said worriedly.

'Yes, I need ice to take the swelling flow down, but the power is out everywhere, and I don't think we'll find any ice here. I'll just put my feet up for now. Let's hope someone comes to find us soon.'

Cassy nodded. And she hoped the same. 'How long will it take them to come and check if anyone is here?'

'It depends. In my opinion, they will first check with drones what the situation is.'

'Can we give them a sign that we are here?' she suggested.

'Yes, I will hang a white flag. In a moment, I will look for something I can use – a towel or a piece of white cloth, but first, I will rest.'

Burke got up, found two more blankets, spread them on the floor, and lay down. Calmed by the drugs he had taken, he slept, and after a few minutes, Cassy heard him snore lightly. Burke's sleep was restless. He talked to himself, and his hands trembled. Cassy watched him for a while, then lay back on the sofa and, like him, tried to sleep, but she couldn't. Her thoughts jumped from worrying about her loved ones to the burning town. Who had done this and why? Burke clearly suspected something, but he didn't want to share it with her. Whoever had prepared the fire had done it very carefully; it had not been an impulsive idea. Someone had been preparing it for days, maybe months. Cassy tried to recall all the criminals in town who could have pulled off such a plan, but no one matched the profile. It had to be someone who worked with and knew about fires or explosives. They also had to be intelligent and have a solid motive to set the city on fire, but not the whole city, just the centre. *Why only the centre?* she wondered. Was anyone guarding the outskirts? Probably someone close to him. But how the hell did he know what to do? How did he know how to control the fires?

A sharp pain in her ankles interrupted her thoughts. Cassy screamed, which woke Burke up. He jumped up quickly and looked at her.

'Where does it hurt?'

'The ankles,' she barely managed to answer.

'I'll look now.'

Burke examined her left leg, then her right. 'Your veins are starting to swell. I need to take you to the hospital urgently.'

Cassy shook her head. She couldn't speak because of the pain.

'No, let me think,' he said. 'We can't go to the other cities, because the road goes through the town centre. We need to call for help from somewhere else, somewhere on the outskirts. Think, you too, Cassy. Where can we go? In one of the houses, I saw a car; the keys were on one of the tables. Think where there might be someone to help us.'

'The lodge,' she whispered softly.

'The lodge? Which lodge?' Burke asked.

'Sam's lodge.'

'Where is this lodge located?'

Cassy, however, could not speak. The pain from her ankles was so bad that she curled up into a ball.

'The lodge,' said Burke thoughtfully, and quickly entered the next room, where a large map of the area was hung.

'Cassy –' He returned to her. 'Show me the lodge.'

Burke almost forcibly lifted her head, making her look at the map. Her gaze was taken, so he took one of the bottles he had brought and sprayed her with water.

'Cassy, last-ditch effort. Where is Sam's lodge located?'

Cassy tried to get up but couldn't. Burke opened the map and started pointing.

'Give me directions. To where? Here?'

Cassy shook her head.

'Here?'

She shook her head again. However, her eyes were fixed on one point. Burke followed her gaze and saw the sign for a lodge.

'It's here, isn't it?'

She nodded, then leaned back and curled up into a ball. Burke stood up, put on the men's slippers he had given her, and left the Sports Centre. After a few minutes, he came back, and even though it was warm, he wrapped Cassy in all the blankets he could find and carried her to the car he had taken.

Then he went back for the water and medicine. He had found food in the three houses and put it in the trunk. With the map in hand, Burke drove the car and prayed a spark wouldn't set it on fire. It was very risky for them to travel now, but it was Cassy's only chance to live, at least according to him.

Cassy woke up to the smell of surgical spirit. Someone was leaning over her, cleaning her face.

'Don't worry. Everything is fine. I'm just cleaning your wounds.'

Cassy tried to open her eyes but couldn't. She could feel the breath of the person helping her, but she couldn't see him.

'Burke brought you two hours ago. He doesn't look good either, you know, but you'll both be fine. I called for help, and they promised to send an ambulance as soon as possible, but I guess they will wait until the morning. The way here is steep and dark; they will hardly risk coming now. My name is Sam, by the way.'

Cassy nodded. So, Burke had managed to get them to the lodge. She only remembered part of the trip. Burke had given her painkillers twice to ease her pain. The second time, he wasn't looking well himself and had told her he was going to pull over to the side of the road to get some rest.

'Let's see what's in here,' Sam said and began to unwrap the bandages that Burke had used to cover her wounds. 'Good. We'll be fine with that too,' he said, then heaved a heavy sigh.

'I found out what happened in Balkan. I hope no other people are hurt,' he said as he put ointment on her palms.

'I hope so too,' Cassy whispered. It still hurt to speak, so she didn't say anything else.

'Don't talk. I'll clean your wounds, then I'll make you tea and soup. You must eat something. Then you can go back to sleep until the ambulance comes to pick you up.'

Cassy managed to pull herself up slightly, straining one eye open and staring at the man in front of her. He hadn't recognized her. The wounds on her face were probably more serious than she thought.

'Sam,' she whispered, 'do you have any more of that herbal tea you make us every time Charlie and I come over?'

The man turned, and surprise was written all over his face.

'Cassy? Cassy Silver, is that you? You don't look like yourself, girl. What happened to you? Where is Charlie?'

'I don't know where he is,' answered Cassy. She could barely get the words out, but she needed to share her fears with someone.

'And what about Steve? Where is your husband?'

'He went to Marta's for a few days.'

Sam walked over to her and stroked her hair gently. 'We will find out what happened to Charlie, and we will call Steve right now to reassure him that you are here. Rest now. Keep your strength.'

Sam walked away and picked up his phone. Cassy waited to hear what Steve had to say, but from Sam's reaction, she knew he hadn't been able to get through to him.

'I'll call him again in a few minutes,' said the lodge host, and he headed for the kitchen.

Cassy looked around the room Sam had put her in. There were two beds in it; Burke was sleeping on the next one. Had he at least been able to contact his relatives? Cassy didn't know if he was married. She looked at his hands and saw the wedding ring. Now that she thought about it, Cassy realized she knew nothing about the short man who had saved her life. All she knew was that he had moved to Balkan after a major accident at work in the capital. She had never seen him outside of town hall meetings. There was no occasion for them to talk outside the office. She didn't even know how old he was, or whether he had any children. His family must be worried about him now.

Cassy's thoughts turned to Steve. There's no way he wouldn't have known about the Balkan fire. Why didn't he pick up the phone? If she were in his place, she would anxiously await every call.

Sam's return with a teapot and two cups interrupted her thoughts.

'The tea will do you good,' he said, and woke Burke. 'You need to eat. After that, if you want, you can sleep until morning.'

Cassy took the warm cup with her bandaged hands and realized that, for the first time in a long time, she felt cold. High in the mountains, the temperatures were always lower. She noticed that Sam had put frozen vegetable packs on her ankles, and the pain in her legs had lessened.

Cassy watched Burke as he sipped his tea. She wanted to thank him for bringing her here, but realized she didn't have the strength to speak. She would do it another time. Burke seemed to sense her gaze and turned to her. He looked at her and nodded in satisfaction.

'You look better,' he said.

Cassy nodded and continued to carefully sip the warm tea. She had wrapped her bandaged hands around the cup.

'And now the soup,' said Sam. He handed a bowl to Burke. Then, with a second ball, he moved to Cassy and began to feed her. She protested at first, but after trying and failing to grab the spoon, she finally let the old man do it.

'Sometimes you just have to accept someone else's help,' he told her gently. After they finished dinner, Sam stood up, took all the utensils, and bade them good night. She lay down on the bed and curled up in a ball, and Burke seemed to fall asleep immediately. He was obviously very tired. *And how could he not be after everything he's been through*? she thought.

-Chapter Four-

The One Who Is Missing

Cassy awoke to voices coming from the entrance of the lodge.

'Where are they?' someone asked.

'In that room,' answered Sam, and she heard the footsteps of people approaching.

A medical team of three people – one man and two women – entered the room. The man went to Cassy's bed, and one of the women to Burke's.

'Cassandra? Is that your name?' asked the doctor.

Cassy nodded. She was unable to speak. Her lips were dry and seemed to stick together.

'I am Doctor Lavrov. I will examine you now. Please stay calm.'

Cassy nodded again and waited for the doctor to examine her injuries. He scowled at almost every wound he saw. Then he turned to the woman who was waiting to the side and told her to bring him some medicine. The other woman called him, and they both hurried out of the room. A minute later, they came back, each with a syringe in their hands, and the nurse named Lisa was carrying an IV. They inserted it into Cassy's better arm and gave her fluids. She calmed down, realizing she was in good hands. Whatever they had given her made her relax quickly, and she felt herself begin to drift off and fall asleep again.

She woke up the next day in the hospital. The doctors and nurses stopped by her room, sometimes talking to her briefly, telling her everything was going to be okay, but not giving her any information about how serious her condition was. Cassy expected to see Steve by her bedside every time she woke up; however, he was not there. On the second day, when she woke up, she saw Eleonora sitting in the chair by her bed. Her sister-in-law had been looking at some documents and hadn't realized yet that Cassy was awake. There were blue circles under her eyes, and her lips were pursed with tension.

'Hey,' Cassy said.

Eleonora looked up, then pushed aside the papers, stood up, and walked over to her.

'Hi,' she said. 'I was worried about you.'

Cassy nodded. 'What do the doctors say?'

'You will be fine. You'll be here for a while, but the important thing is that you don't have any complications, and you probably won't even have any scars afterwards.'

'Great.' Cassy sighed with relief. 'Where's Steve?'

'I don't know.'

'How come you don't know? Isn't he here?' Cassy whispered. It was hard for her to speak, but she had to know what was going on.

'No, he didn't come.'

Cassy looked at her sister-in-law in confusion.

'No one has seen him for several days.'

'Doesn't your mother know where he is? The last I heard from him was that he was with her.' Cassy gasped, feeling pain as she spoke, and slumped back against the pillow. Eleonora walked over to her and stroked her hair gently. Her look was concerned.

'He's not with her. I'm sorry, Cassy. I do not know what to tell you. I'm looking for him too. I'm very worried, but we can't find him at the moment.'

Cassy swallowed hard. She had a hard time asking her next question. 'What about Charlie?'

'We can't find him either.'

Cassy's eyes watered. Her husband wasn't here when she needed him, and her dog was probably lost, or worse, dead.

'Your parents are here. They stayed with me. They will come to see you as soon as I get home.'

'At least they are concerned about me,' Cassy said sadly.

'Hey, don't do that. My family loves you too. The kids keep asking about you. They miss you. And Marta said she'd visit you as soon as we found Steve. She is very worried about him right now.'

'Sorry, I probably sound selfish. Of course, I'm worried about him too.' Cassy thought about the fire and looked Eleonora in the eye. 'Did you find out who set fire to the town?'

'You think someone deliberately started the fire?' Her sister-in-law was surprised.

'Isn't that right?'

'As far as I know from the fire department report, it was an accident.'

'Okay,' said Cassy, realizing she probably said something she shouldn't. The doubts were Burke's; he should have talked to Eleonora about it, not she.

'Rest now,' said her sister-in-law. 'I will go home and send a car to bring your parents here.'

Eleonora looked at her, opened her lips as if to say something else, but then hurriedly gathered up her papers and belongings, kissed Cassy on the forehead, and hurried out of the room.

Cassy followed Eleonora with her gaze. The door slammed loudly after her sister-in-law left, and it gave her a headache. She cowered and stared at the window. She kept forgetting to ask where she was. She was hardly in the hospital in Balkan. She was probably in Rhodopa, the larger neighbouring town. Cassy had come here with Steve several times for a romantic dinner. However, romance had long since left them both. No matter how many flowers he'd bought her, no matter how many dinners he'd taken her out to, or she'd made for him, something had broken between the two of them, and it was clear to Cassy that he wasn't coming anytime soon. It was the last straw they could grasp at to save their marriage, but Steve hadn't taken it. Now she felt lonely. Without him and Charlie, her life once again would become what it was before – lonely. *Where are they both now?* she wondered.

Cassy looked at the bedside table and noticed several cards and bouquets. She started to reach out and see who they were from, but the pain in her arms and back stopped her. She rose slightly and extended her hand to them. The moment she took one of the cards in her hand, she heard the door open. On her doorstep stood a short woman of delicate beauty. Cassy had never seen her before. The woman approached her bed.

'I am Berta, Burke's wife,' she said quietly and looked at the woman in front of her.

'Your husband saved my life,' Cassy said and tried to smile.

'I know. He told me what happened. I came to see how you are.' Berta looked at Cassy again, but her look was not one of pity. 'Actually, I came to tell you something.'

Cassy looked at her questioningly.

'My husband almost died because of you. I can't believe a police chief would risk her life for a dog. *A dog!* My husband would not have these wounds and be in this condition if it were not for you and your selfishness.'

Cassy looked at the woman in amazement. 'I did not know ...'

'What didn't you know? Your neighbour told you your dog wasn't there, but you still went inside. I almost lost my husband because of you.'

As she said all this, tears fell from Berta's eyes. She wiped them nervously and started to leave the room.

'Berta,' Cassy called.

The petite woman turned.

'This dog is the closest being in my life. The only thing I really love.'

Berta stared at her, then nodded slightly and hurried out of the room, and Cassy took a deep breath, amazed at what she had just said to her. Was Charlie really the most important one in her life? Shouldn't that be a person, someone she loved and trusted, like a mother, a father, a brother, a husband? Unwittingly, Cassy had told the truth. She loved no one else the way she loved her dog. It was difficult for even her to understand it; how could she explain it to anyone else? She looked out of the window again and wondered why Steve had lied to her. If he hadn't gone to his mother's, he might actually have been able to get into the flat and take Charlie. But that would mean he hadn't even left town. She had to get up and find him. Cassy tried to get up again. This time, she harnessed all her strength and finally succeeded. She opened the drawer of the nightstand, hoping her phone would be there, but didn't find it. She was just about to try to sit up when she heard the door to the room open. This time, it was her neighbour Marina. Cassy rested her head on the pillow and stared at the old woman. Marina was a Russian who had moved to Balkan many years ago. She knew almost everyone in town and was an inexhaustible source of information that Cassy often tapped into.

'You don't look good,' said her neighbour.

'I'll be fine.'

'Let's hope it will be soon. There are a lot of robbed houses in town, and everyone hopes you'll get back to work soon and find the thieves.'

'Are there any other victims besides Burke and me?'

'As far as I know, only you have suffered severely,' said Marina, but from her look, it was clear that she wanted to say something more.

'You can tell me,' Cassy encouraged her.

'Steve is gone. I come here every few hours to see how you are, but I haven't met him even once.'

'I know. Eleonora said they were looking for him. They're also looking for Charlie.'

'I told you not to enter the block, but you didn't listen to me. Steve took Charlie. I saw him with my own eyes.'

'I know, Marina. I believe you now, but then I had reason to doubt it.'

'Do you have any idea where he is?'

Cassy didn't answer right away, thinking about what to say to her.

'No, I have no idea where he is. He may be trying to call me, but I don't have a phone. I left my work phone at the police station before the fire, and it probably burned, and I think I lost my personal phone in the mountain.' Cassy was talking, but at one point, she felt faint and closed her eyes. She hated feeling helpless.

Marina walked over to the bed and looked at her.

'I will ask Michael to bring you a new one,' she said. Michael was her nephew, and he ran an electronics store in town.

'I would be very grateful to you,' said Cassy, and made a sign that she was tired.

'Do you need anything else?' Marina asked.

'No. Thanks for visiting me. Not many people would do that after such a disaster.' Then she closed her eyes and felt tears running down her cheeks. Marina came close to her and gently wiped them away.

'Everything will be fine,' she said, then slowly left the room.

Cassy relaxed and went back to sleep. She awoke to muffled voices close to her and opened her eyes to see her parents sitting on the two chairs beside her bed. They were quietly debating whether to make her move in with them or let her stay in the hospital for a while longer. Cassy's parents always tried to make decisions for her. That was the problem in her relationship with them. They tried to control her, and this always led to arguments, and after the arguments, their relationship always cooled. Cassy had a feeling the same thing was about to happen now, so she just closed her eyes and let her parents argue.

When she woke up, they were no longer there. To her surprise, Burke was sitting in the chair next to her bed, reading something in a folder. He was so engrossed in what was written inside that he didn't realize that Cassy had woken up. She watched him for a while, trying to understand what was written in the document.

'Hey,' she said.

He looked up in surprise to see Cassy watching him and smiled at her.

'Hey. I came to see how you are. How do you feel? Any better?'

'I'm fine. Thanks for saving me.'

'It's my job.'

'I know, but still, I would like to say thank you. Shouldn't you be resting too?' she asked and looked at his leg and the still-unhealed wounds on his arms.

'I should, but I'm feeling better and decided to go over the reports.'

'Is there something interesting?'

'No. As I assumed, there were six fires, but it is not yet known who set them and why. Tomorrow, I will voluntarily discharge myself from the hospital and go inspect the places before all traces and evidence are gone.'

'You didn't tell the mayor about your suspicions, did you?'

'No. I want to be sure before I talk to her.'

'I told her, but she ignored me. Sorry, I thought you had discussed it with her.'

'Don't worry about it,' Burke said, but Cassy saw a glimmer of concern in his eyes.

'Where are we?' she asked.

'What?' He did not understand her question.

'Which hospital are we in?'

'In the municipal hospital in Rhodope. I thought you knew where you were.'

'No, I didn't know. The doctors don't tell me anything.'

'I was told that you need a few more days of rest. Then you can go home.'

Cassy looked at him, and he saw confusion in her eyes.

'What's bothering you?'

'My apartment burned down. I wonder where to go after, you know ...'

'And our house is affected by the fire. Berta is having a nervous breakdown. We were given temporary housing in the upper part of the town. I guess they will give you one too. Marina mentioned that you could stay with your sister-in-law. She said you two are very close.'

'Yes, we are close, but I prefer right now to be further away from Steve's family.'

'He didn't come, did he?' Burke asked.

'No, he didn't come, and no one knows where he is.' Cassy shook her head sadly. 'Have you heard anything about him?'

'No, but tomorrow, as soon as I see his colleagues, I will question them. I will let you know if they know something. Don't worry, everything will be fine. Now you have to rest and recover.'

'Yes, I have no choice, right?' Cassy said. 'Marina mentioned that there were many robberies after the fire.'

'Probably so. I was convinced that someone would take advantage of the situation,' said Burke and sighed heavily. Then he got up from the chair. 'Rest, Cassy. Call me when you get out of the hospital.'

'I definitely will. And Burke ...'

'Yes?'

'Tell your wife I'm sorry. She came to see me.'

'I know. Berta told me she lost her temper. She has been through a lot. This town doesn't seem to be for her. She just decided that people were starting to accept us, and that's what happened. She had put a lot of energy into the house.'

'Do you have any children?'

'Yes. Two girls.'

Cassy nodded. Burke turned and walked slowly to the door.

'Burke ...'

'Yes?'

'You know who set fire to the city, don't you?'

He turned to her, his gaze briefly studying her face as if trying to unravel something.

'I don't know who did it, but even if I knew, I wouldn't tell you right now. First, I have to go and inspect the burned-out places.'

'Okay,' Cassy said uncertainly. Something told her that he didn't trust her and that his gaze meant something else. Burke suspected her of something, and she didn't know what it was.

'Now rest,' he said, and he left the room, limping.

Cassy's gaze remained fixed on the closed door. Burke's words and behaviour puzzled her. She tried to piece together the events and find something that connected her to this fire, but nothing came to mind. Finally, she fell asleep, exhausted.

She dreamed of Ron, her first husband. Ron was the only human Cassy had ever madly loved. They had met at the police academy. At first, the two could not stand each other; they were always arguing and insulting each other. However, it quickly turned into passion and grew into mutual trust and understanding. She and Ron were married right after graduating from the police academy. They had decided to advance their careers for a few years and then have children. But that never happened. Two years after their marriage, Ron died of his wounds in a shootout. It took Cassy several years and many sleepless nights to get over her loss, or rather, come to terms with it. But she often dreamed of him, especially in important moments for her.

'Get up,' he told her in her sleep.

'Why should I get up?' she asked.

'Get up,' he insisted.

'But why?'

He didn't answer. He just stroked her hair gently and left where he had come from.

Cassy woke up drenched in sweat. It was hard for her to breathe; she could barely catch her breath. Then she realized someone was pressing a pillow over her face and trying to suffocate her. She tried to free herself and dug her claws into her assailant's arms. This caused him to back away. She managed briefly to push the pillow aside and take a deep breath. The person attacking her continued to put the pillow on top of her face but had already lost his balance. Cassy could hear his breathing. The two of them wrestled until something fell from the bedside table and smashed noisily into pieces on the floor. Frightened, her assailant backed away quickly and headed for the door. Just before exiting, he threw the pillow that was still in his hands in Cassy's direction. She tried to catch it and thus missed the moment when she could see his face in the light coming from the corridor. Her attacker had slipped out before the doctor on call entered her room. All Cassy could make out was that it was a man. She could sense this as she struggled with it. He smelled strange, maybe mechanical. Why did he try to choke her, Cassy wondered. Why would anyone want to kill her?

After checking everything in her hospital room, the hospital management and the local police decided to assign security to her. Cassy watched the policeman standing outside her room and kept wondering who wanted to kill her and why. She stayed awake until morning. Finally tired of the dark thoughts and mixed feelings, she fell asleep and dreamed of him again.

'Stay here,' Ron told her. 'Don't go there.'

'Where should I not go?' she asked him. He did not answer, but he left, and she felt abandoned again.

Cassy opened her eyes, expecting to see her husband, but the chair was empty. There was no one in the room. She took a deep breath. What had happened that night had shaken her. Every time she tried to close her eyes, she saw flames around her or pillows pressing her to the bed. She took the pillow from the bed and threw it at the door. Her breathing had sped up from the stress, and the equipment she was attached to started beeping. A nurse hastily entered the room, who, looking in Cassy's direction, did not notice the pillow thrown on the floor, tripped over it, and fell. Cassy watched the woman, reached out to help her up, but a sharp pain sent her back to bed.

'I'm so sorry,' she said to the nurse, who had already stood again. 'Just looking at the pillow makes me sick.'

The woman rubbed her knees and gave Cassy a reassuring smile. Then she approached the equipment, looked at something, and left the room.

After the nurse closed the door, Cassy managed to sit up in bed and began examining her arms and legs. Her hands were still bandaged, and so were her ankles. The rest of her body wasn't badly hurt. She had scars from the bushes and branches on her upper arms as well as her thighs, but the wounds were no longer red and had begun to heal. Cassy looked away from her body and stared at the cards left on her bedside table. Most were from relatives and acquaintances, but one of them made an impression on her.

I'm sorry

S.

Nothing else was written in it. There was no get-well wish, and Cassy wondered who had left that card. Was it Steve or someone else with the same initials? She took it in her hands again and examined it more closely. The card was not a design that Steve would have chosen. There were no flowers or bright colours. It was a simple card; her husband was into more impressive things, something to attract attention. And the handwriting wasn't his. Someone else had left a private message for Cassy. The question was *who*? Who but Steve would do that?

The opening of the door interrupted her thoughts. Eleonora entered the room. Her face looked tired, and her smile was languid and somewhat artificial. Cassy turned to her sister-in-law and did her best to hide the card under the blanket. She didn't know why she did this, but her actions were prompted by her intuition, and it hadn't lied to her before.

'I see you got rid of the pillow.'

'Yes. I had nightmares all the time and decided it was better not to have it near me.'

'How are you?' Eleonora asked her.

'I am better. Today, I will try to get up and walk. If I can stay on my feet longer and not feel pain from the burn wounds, I'll probably be able to go home tomorrow or the day after.'

'You know your flat burned down, right?' Eleonora said and looked at her quizzically.

'Of course I know. I was there when part of the block was in flames.'

'You can stay with me and help me with the twins,' suggested Eleonora. 'The babysitter left town, and now I'm looking for a new one. Your parents are looking after them right now, but I can tell from their faces that they want to go.'

'I hope you don't get upset, but I would like to live somewhere else alone. I need to recover from what happened.'

'Okay, but you will still have to stay with me for a few days until a vacant place suitable for you is found. Half the city has burned down, and there aren't many free places. Those we had, we distributed to families with children.'

'Okay,' Cassy agreed, although she didn't like the idea of living with her sister-in-law very much. 'Any news on Steve?'

'We only found out that he left town with Charlie. One of your neighbours brought them here to the Rhodope, and from here, all traces are lost. His phone goes straight to voicemail.'

'What time was it when he left the town?' Cassy asked, trying to make a timeframe.

'An hour after the first explosion.'

'I was trying to cross the bridge then. We probably crossed paths somewhere there.'

'Probably,' Eleonora said, then reached into her purse, pulled out two phones, and handed them to Cassy.

'I checked the messages. He really texted you that he was at our mother's.'

Cassy was amazed. 'Have you been checking my private messages?'

'Yes. My brother is missing, and you were the last person he talked to.'

"That doesn't give you the right to check my calls and messages. You know it's illegal, right?'

'I know. Sorry, but I was really worried about Steve.'

Cassy entered the password into her personal phone and looked at the recent messages. There was no news from her husband or anyone else. However, there were many new emails, voicemails, and text messages on her work phone. Cassy thought she'd better listen to them after her sister-in-law left.

'Tell my parents I'm not coming back to live with them. I would like to stay with you until a place becomes available for me and for ...' She didn't finish. Did she have a husband and a pet? she wondered, and felt a void in her feelings. The only one she was missing right now was Charlie. Cassy turned to Eleonora and wondered if she missed her husband. Now they both had the same fate – their husbands had left them and disappeared.

-Chapter Five-

Why?

Two days later, Cassy left the hospital. Eleonora had come in her private car to pick her up, and the twins were also with her.

'We will drop you off at home, and then I will take them to school,' said her sister-in-law as she handed Cassy a bottle of water. 'The doctor recommended drinking plenty of fluids.'

Cassy took the bottle and drank some of the water. It tasted slightly bitter.

'Cassy, does it hurt a lot?' Rita asked.

'No, nothing hurts.'

'Can we see the scars?' asked Bobo in turn.

'You will have to see them; won't I live in your house?'

'Yes, true.' Rita smiled happily. 'We're going to have a girls' party. We'll get a manicure, and maybe I'll do your hair.'

Cassy laughed and enjoyed the childish enthusiasm. She hadn't done her hair and manicure in a long time; maybe it was time to take care of her appearance.

'Drink water,' Eleonora encouraged her again. Cassy lifted the bottle but only took one sip. The liquid inside smelled like something burned. All that smoke she had inhaled during and after the fire had probably affected her senses.

The distance between Balkan and Rhodope was not great, and in just forty-five minutes, the four arrived at Eleonora's house. Cassy's parents had left early in the morning, making sure to stop by to see her at the hospital. After a brief argument, it became clear to everyone that Cassy would not be going with them, and they left again, disappointed in her. Whatever she did, it wasn't right for them. Cassy swallowed loudly at the memory of the conversation with her parents. Then she opened the car door and struggled to enter her sister-in-law's large house. Eleonora had already opened the front door and was carrying Cassy's luggage inside.

'You can look in my closet and choose some clothes. As soon as you get better, and I find more free time, we'll go shopping for anything else you need.'

'Thank you,' Cassy said and felt her sight darken. She felt sick. 'I'll use the toilet, and then I'll go to bed,' she added, waved goodbye to the children, and locked herself in the bathroom. She splashed water on her face and sat on the small chair next to the tub. Her phone rang, and she looked at the display. It was an unknown number. *Maybe it's Steve*, she thought, and quickly picked up.

'Cassy?' She heard Burke's voice.

'Yes.'

'I went to the hospital, but they told me that they had discharged you. I want to show you something.'

'Okay. Come to Eleonora's house.'

Burke was silent for a moment, then agreed and asked her to dictate the address to him. Cassy wondered what Burke wanted to show her. She tried to think, but dark-grey clouds seemed to settle in her head. She stood up and splashed cold water on her face. Then she left the bathroom and lay down on the sofa in the hallway. Her legs did not support her, her head was heavy, and her body was limp. *Something is wrong with me*, she thought. At that moment, she heard the doorbell ring. Then someone began knocking insistently on the door, but Cassy didn't have the strength to get up. She tried to stand or say something but couldn't. Her head felt heavy, and despite her efforts to stay awake, she felt herself drifting off. Then she heard someone calling her name, and it made her open her eyes. She saw the silhouette of a man enter and heard him speak to her. Cassy tried to say something, to ask who it was, but she felt lost and seemed to be losing consciousness. Someone grabbed her shoulders and shook her. She looked up at him and saw Ron's face in a blur. *Is he alive?* she wondered. He can't be alive. Ron is dead, she told herself, and she felt herself drifting off into darkness.

Cassy woke up a few hours later in the small makeshift emergency hospital at the bottom of Balkan. She looked around and saw several people milling about in the large common room. Besides her, there were four more beds with patients. She knew the doctor, who now stood with his back to her, as well as the nurse. Cassy had spoken to them often in some of the violent cases she investigated as police chief.

The room they were in was new, and it smelled of fresh paint. Cassy saw three doors, one with a restroom sign, and she tried to get up and head there. Her movement caused the medics to turn around.

'Don't get up.' Doctor Fisher stopped her and approached her. Cassy only now noticed that there was an IV attached to her right arm.

'I want to go to the toilet,' she said. The doctor gently laid her down and removed the needle from the cannula that had been attached to her.

'Okay, I'll help you stand up now,' he said and grabbed her by the waist. Cassy couldn't stand steadily on her feet, so she lay back and accepted the doctor's help.

'What happened? Why am I here?' she asked as they shortened the distance to the door.

'I'll tell you in a moment. Maggie, help Cassy,' he said, and let the nurse tend to her.

After leaving the toilet, Cassy headed to the doctor.

'What's wrong with me? Why did I pass out?'

'Sit here,' said Dr Fisher, placing her in a chair near his desk. 'What do you remember?' he asked.

'I remember entering Eleonora's house, and then it dawned on me. Someone rang the doorbell, then came in ...'

'Burke has come to see you. He said you were supposed to meet at the house.'

'That's right.'

'He found you almost unconscious, lying on the sofa.'

'So, it was him.'

'Yes. He saved your life.'

'Right?' Cassy was surprised.

'Yes. The tests show a small dose of nicotine in your body. The dose was enough to knock you out in a few hours. Do you remember what you had for breakfast, what you drank this morning?'

'I didn't have breakfast. I drank tea... I actually didn't drink tea; they just brought it to me, but I didn't drink it.'

'You took that nicotine with something. Have you had any unusual procedure, injection, or pill, something with a bitter taste?'

'Water ...' Cassy muttered quietly.

'What?' Doctor Fisher didn't understand what she said.

'Water. I drank water. Eleonora gave me a bottle of still water and told me that the doctors recommended that I drink more fluids.'

'Where is the water bottle now?'

'I do not know. I don't remember where I left it; it's probably at her house.' Cassy tried to remember where she last saw the bottle, but she couldn't. 'I really don't remember. I will ask Eleonora to check that it is not left in her car. I don't remember taking it with me because the water tasted strange to me.'

'If it's still in the car, I'll send someone to go get it. Tell me the address of the house.'

Cassy dictated it to him.

'Doctor Fisher, are you saying that someone tried to poison me this morning?'

'Yes. I'm sorry, but apparently, there is someone out there who wants you dead. And not only you.'

Cassy was trying to make sense of what Doctor Fisher had said. Why should someone want to kill her? And not only her?

'Who else are they trying to kill?'

'Burke. Today at noon, they shot at him.'

'What? Is he okay?'

'Yes. Burke is fine. Now he's sending his wife and daughters to her parents' house. What's going on, Cassy? What did you and Burke get involved in?'

'Honestly, I have no idea. Whatever it is, it must be something they're willing to kill us for.'

'I think they are well organized. There is no way one person could do all this.'

'Isn't it too early to jump to conclusions?' Cassy asked.

'Before I moved here, I worked in the emergency department in one of the most criminal-ridden districts in the capital. Believe me, I have an intuition about these things.' The doctor spoke in a whisper.

'Where is Burke now?' Cassy asked.

'Probably traveling with his family. He said not to call him and that he would come and talk to you as soon as he got back.'

'Okay. Do I have to stay here, or can I go?' she asked, looking at the IV next to her bed.

'I would recommend you stay until Burke comes. You are safe in the clinic; no one but me and Maggie comes in here.'

'Aren't you going to rest?'

'We rested for two days. I personally won't leave here until I'm sure you're all right and safe. By the way, your deputy, Zlotov, wants to talk to you. He said to call him as soon as you wake up.'

'Thanks, Fisher. I owe you.'

'You're welcome,' said the doctor and retreated to the improvised laboratory.

Cassy got up and slowly walked over to her bed. However, her legs still wouldn't hold her, and Maggie came to help her. After settling into the bed, Cassy picked up her work phone and called Zlotov.

'Boss, are you okay?' asked the young man, concern in his voice.

'I am fine. How is it at police headquarters?'

'Uh ... the police headquarters is ...' Zlotov began to stammer.

'Yes, of course. I haven't been through the city yet and forgot about it. Where is everyone now? I guess they gave us temporary accommodation.'

'Yes, they accommodated us in the Sports Centre at the upper end of the city. If the rumours are true, you and Burke were in it looking for the first-aid kit.'

'Yes, we were there. How is the situation? Any problems besides robberies?'

'You know about the robberies?' Zlotov was surprised.

'I have my sources.' Cassy smiled.

'Okay. I assume you also know about the Burke shooting.'

'Yes, I was notified. Any suspects?'

'No, we still don't know who planned this.'

'Will you bring me the reports on all of the cases?' Cassy asked. She had to be on to something. It would distract her from the feeling of helplessness that had come over her.

'Of course, boss. Where can I bring them to you?'

'I'm with Doctor Fisher and Maggie.'

'Okay. I will come as soon as possible.'

'See you soon,' Cassy said.

'See you soon,' replied her deputy.

Zlotov was Marina's other nephew. He was young and green but conscientious and kind-hearted. Cassy had hired him right after he graduated from the police academy. He was the other source of information about the people in town that Cassy used, though the young man didn't realize it. Zlotov knew almost everyone. He was also very aware of the criminals in Balkan because he had been one of them before. His love for Maggie had changed him. The young girl, now working as a nurse, had captured his heart. It was beautiful to watch them talk. They were like two lovebirds. Cassy didn't miss the slight smile on Maggie's face when she found out her boyfriend was coming to visit. And he did not delay; half an hour later, Zlotov appeared with a small tablet and several folders under his arm.

'Let's see what you brought me,' Cassy said excitedly, and she impatiently reached for the documents.

'First the robberies,' said Zlotov. 'Because different items were taken, I assume that they were committed by several people, not just one.'

'Do you have suspects?' Cassy asked, knowing very well that he already knew who had stolen what. Stealing was his strength. He knew the style of every thief in town, which was why he was one of her most valuable recruits, and for that reason, she had promoted him to deputy, ignoring his older colleagues. Cassy had made a risky decision then, but she never regretted it.

'I know who took the jewellery. I know who took the drugs as well, but I have no idea who stole the blueprints from the Archive Warehouse.'

Who needs these documents? Cassy asked herself.

'Exactly. Why would anyone bother doing that? He can just request them.'

'Where is the Archive Warehouse? Isn't it at the edge of town?'

'Yes. And you know what else is weird? Whoever he was, he was there during – or shortly after – the fire. There was soot and ash on the parquet. The other thefts were committed before then, and the thieves sped off and left town. However, this thief left around the time of the fire.'

'Interesting. Were you able to get any prints off?'

'No. Only the soot and ash remain on the laminate and are exactly where I think the folders are missing.'

'Is there anything else missing?' Cassy asked, puzzled.

'The staff there are currently checking, but for now, that is all.'

'How many folders are missing?'

'So far, we know about eight.'

'Something to do with gas or electricity?'

'No, just plans of buildings, some of them empty for decades.'

'Um ... okay. Now tell me about Burke.'

'What exactly do you want to know?' asked Zlotov, and he sat down on the toilet. The two of them had entered the narrow room so that no one could hear what they were talking about.

'Everything you know about him,' Cassy said, and she leaned back in the chair they had brought in. Her whole body ached, especially the hand where the cannula had been inserted, but she tried not to let the pain get the better of her and focused on the information her colleague was giving her.

'His name is Burke Pastry, but everyone calls him by his first name, even his bosses. Burke was very good at his job in the capital, but his ascent to a bigger career stalled after a major accident at a sugar factory where three of his best friends died.'

'What happened there?'

'I only know rumours; I have no official information.'

'That works for me.'

'Okay. The owner altered a large part of the factory without new planning permission. Accordingly, when Burke and his colleagues entered the burning factory, they had only the old plan of the building. Three of them ended up in the cauldrons of melting sugar instead of in the offices. Have you seen how sugar melts?' asked Zlotov.

'I have seen,' Cassy said, and understood why the young man did not want to continue. At higher temperatures, sugar liquefies and turns into caramel, then slowly begins to burn and release black fumes, that can quickly suffocate you. Finally, everything burns and turns into a solid black mass, like cold lava, which is difficult to separate from any surface. If Burke's colleagues had gotten into that sugar container, they most likely would have turned into just that, black baked sugar. Cassy felt sick at the thought.

'What else do you know?' she asked, trying not to think about black smoke and soot.

'Burke is happily married with two children.'

'Two daughters, right?'

'Yes. He moved to Balkan two years ago, exactly one year after the incident with his friends.'

'I can't help but ask you,' Cassy said, 'do you think he stole the documents from the Archive Warehouse?'

'I don't know, Cassy, but he's suspicious. He acts like he knows something we don't.'

So Zlotov had sensed this too, she thought. 'Anything else about him? Brothers? Sisters? Any relatives?'

'He has a brother and a sister, but as far as we know, they are not in touch.'

'Who is he in touch with from his old life?'

'With his boss, a retired firefighter. But he lives five hundred miles from here. As far as I know, they hear from each other once a week and email each other occasionally.'

'There has to be something else,' Cassy whispered.

'I didn't find anything else about him, boss.'

'Okay, keep asking. But don't make it obvious; I don't want to hurt his ego. He saved my life twice, though.'

'Twice?' Zlotov was surprised.

'Yes. Someone tried to poison me this morning and put liquid nicotine in my bottle of still water.'

'What? I was told by Doctor Fisher and Maggie that you probably passed out from the burns, and that's why you're under observation at the hospital. Will you be okay?'

'Yes. I'll be fine. Tomorrow morning, I will come to the new police station, and we will work on all these cases. Now I feel tired.'

'Okay, boss, I'll let you rest. Shall I leave the folders for you to look through?'

'Yes, there is nothing else for me to do.'

She got up, but then sat down again and motioned for him to stay too.

'Steve is missing,' she whispered. 'He took Charlie, and we don't know where he is.'

'I thought he was with his mother,' said Zlotov and looked at her with a sympathetic look, similar to the one Marina had given her. Cassy hated being seen as a victim.

'Who told you that Steve is at his mother's?' she asked.

'Eleonora mentioned to me when I asked her if he was coming to see you.'

'He's not at Marta's. Eleonora said they don't know where he is. They're looking for him.'

'But why didn't she tell me?' Zlotov's astonishment was visible. As her deputy, the mayor was supposed to notify him if there was a missing person.

'You know what, that's what I'm asking myself. Maybe she doesn't want anyone in town to know about it.'

'Or she knows where he is ...' Zlotov swallowed loudly, realizing that he had said something wrong.

'Yes,' Cassy agreed. 'I'm going to make a call or two, but in the meantime, I'm going to ask you to request the phone transcript of Steve's calls from his personal phone. Report him missing on my request. Also, write information about Charlie.'

'Are you sure, boss? The mayor might not agree with that.'

'I'm sure. Steve is my husband, and I don't know where he is. No one has seen or heard from him for several days. He also took our dog with him. I have every right to declare him missing and start an investigation.'

'Okay,' he said, but Cassy could see his concern. Zlotov got up, opened the door, and helped her into bed. Then he took all the folders and the new tablet he had brought her and placed them next to her.

'Rest now,' he said, and made a gesture to Maggie that he was done with the conversation, and they both went outside.

Cassy scanned the room. Dr. Fisher had gone out, and only the patients remained inside. In total, there were two women and two men. They were all staring at the folders next to Cassy. Their curiosity was obvious.

'This is classified information, and I cannot share it with you,' she told them and pulled the folders closer to her. Then she took the top one and read the reports inside. Cassy had been in town long enough to be aware of pickpockets and petty thieves. Zlotov was right; they would quickly find out who did most of the robberies. They already had enough leads and evidence for two of them. She went through all the reports carefully, leaving the one with the missing archival documents for last. There was something strange about this theft. The thief didn't seem to be in a hurry. And the other strange thing was that he had left all the drawers from which he had taken a folder open. It was as if he wanted to show what he had taken. *Or perhaps this is all a front, and he's actually gone for something else*, Cassy wondered. They wouldn't find out about the lack of other documents until a few weeks later. Most people had left the town and, according to Zlotov, everything was happening in slow motion in the city.

'I even have the feeling that in the cafe they make coffee more slowly, which actually makes no sense because the coffee machine they use is the same,' he had said before he left.

Cassy turned back to the folder. Why would anyone want to steal these documents? Why did he risk his life to enter the Archives Warehouse during the fire? Even though the building was located at the upper end of the city, the heat from the burning town was great; Cassy remembered that very well. Whoever had gone in there most likely had similar injuries to hers and

Burke's. Was the firefighter involved? Why would anyone want to shoot him then? And why do they want to kill her too? Why? Why? Why? There were a thousand questions in her head. Cassy saw that Doctor Fisher was back. She was calmed by his presence and lay her head back. Then she closed her eyes, drifted slowly into a doze, and finally fell asleep.

-Chapter Six-

Sometimes It's Better Not to Know the Truth

Cassy awoke to the sound of a muffled conversation. She opened her eyes to see Doctor Fisher and Burke talking animatedly. The two were tense, as if they were arguing about something. She tried to hear what they were talking about, but the man next to her was snoring loudly, and she couldn't hear much. Only partial words reached her. She stood up slightly, and the files she had left near her fell with a crash to the floor. This drew everyone's attention to her. Burke limped over and began picking up the fallen folders. Fisher also tried to help him. Cassy saw Burke's eyes land on the folder with his name on it. He looked up at her and smiled.

'You studied me,' he said.

'I'm sure you did the same.'

He didn't answer, but Cassy knew from his look that she was right.

'How are you?' he asked her after handing her the collected folders.

'Okay. And how are you?'

'I'm fine too,' said Burke, and he looked around nervously. All the patients had raised their heads and were looking at the two of them. 'Maybe it's better to talk somewhere more secluded.'

'There's no lonelier place than the toilet,' Cassy said, and her comment made everyone smile. Burke helped her off the bed, then took all the papers and the tablet and followed her into the small room.

'Can I have a look at my file?' he asked her, amused.

'Of course,' Cassy said and looked at him inquisitively. 'Is there anything inside that you don't know?'

'Yes, you are right. Perhaps it's better I don't look.'

Cassy sat across from him and watched him. She didn't know how to start the conversation, so she did what she always did at times like this and went straight off the deep end.

'Did you steal the documents from the Archive Warehouse?' she asked him as she looked into his face, hoping to see something that would give him away if he had done it.

'What?' His confusion was genuine. 'When? What documents? And where is the Archive Warehouse?'

Cassy continued to look at him, but it was already clear to her that he was not the thief. Her instinct told her that the person who took these documents was the same person who had set the city on fire.

'Sorry, forget what I asked you,' she said, but she knew he wasn't going to let her get away easily.

'No!' he protested. 'You owe me an explanation. I've saved your life twice, and I think you can trust me.'

Cassy remained silent and continued to study his reactions. Of course, he was right; there was no reason not to trust him. She could see on his face how he was first surprised, then intrigued by what she said, and finally angry.

'Sorry, you're right. It's just that everything has happened so fast, like a magician pulling one surprise after another out of his hat.'

'You know what,' said Burke, still looking at her angrily. 'I feel the same way. I had to send my family far away, and all I get from you is doubt. Why do you doubt me? Where is this Archive Warehouse located, and when were these documents stolen? I've researched every public building in the city; I'm just now hearing about the Archive Warehouse.' Burke spoke quickly. At one point, he stopped to catch his breath.

'Relax. I already apologized to you.'

Burke sat on the floor, apparently oblivious to the bacteria living there.

'You don't know about this building because it is part of a house. Two families rent there. There is a two-story building in the yard of the house. You have to enter the house itself to get there.'

'And where is it located?'

'One block from the Sports Centre,' said Cassy. 'According to my colleague, the documents were taken when you and I were there. There are ashes and soot left on the floor. You probably know that after we went up to Sam's lodge, it was drizzling, and helicopters dropped a lot of water over the town. The person who left the tracks had been inside before that.'

Burke looked at Cassy. 'I understand why you suspect me. I was nearby at the time, and I am the perfect suspect.'

'Yes,' she admitted. 'Did you notice anyone else while you were in the area?'

'No, but I haven't looked either. I was busy with other things, but now that I think about it, there were traces in one of the houses I entered. It didn't make much of an impression on me then, but now ...'

'In which house?' Cassy asked.

'We can go tomorrow with your colleague, and I can show it to him,' promised Burke.

'Thank you, and again, sorry for the doubts,' said Cassy sincerely.

'What documents did they steal from the Archive Warehouse?' Burke asked.

'I don't know exactly; I think they are plans of buildings.'

Something changed in Burke's eyes at the mention of building plans. 'Can we find out which buildings?'

'We can. I'm thinking of going to the Archive Warehouse tomorrow and talking to the staff. You can come with me if you want,' she suggested.

'Okay, I'll come with you,' he agreed.

'This morning you wanted to talk to me about something,' she reminded him.

'Yes, but it can wait. You must see something, but I don't have it with me.'

'At least tell me what it is,' Cassy said.

'You will understand the moment you see it,' he answered and stood up. 'I have to go – I've had a long, hard day, and I need some rest.'

'Okay. Come and pick me up tomorrow morning. We'll go to the Archive Warehouse, and then you'll show me what you found.'

'Sounds like a plan.' He smiled slightly.

Burke helped her back to bed again, though she already felt a rush of energy and felt like she didn't need help. He placed the folders and the tablet next to her, smiled at her, and left. Cassy saw Doctor Fisher watching her and motioned for him to come closer.

'What's happening?' she asked him. 'What were you arguing about?'

'It was a dispute between a doctor and a patient,' said Doctor Fisher. 'I can't discuss it with you.'

'You argued about his leg, didn't you? He continues to limp.'

'I can't confirm or deny,' Doctor Fisher said, but he nodded his agreement. Burke was injured and not taking care of himself, Cassy read from Doctor Fisher's nod. She dialled Zlotov's phone and advised him to double the guard on Burke.

'Someone wants him dead, but I don't know why,' she said. Then she leaned back, opened the tablet, and began searching for information about the accident that killed Burke's friends. She read almost everything online about the Balkan fire. Finally, she looked up information about Steve. She wondered if Marta and Eleonora had even looked for him. Had they been covering for him all this time? Even though she knew it was late, she decided to call his mother. Marta picked up almost immediately.

'Cassy, are you okay? I heard you're in the hospital again. How do you feel?'

'I'm fine. According to the doctor, I will recover quickly. How are you?'

'I'm fine too.' Marta's voice was calm. She certainly didn't sound like a worried mother who doesn't know where her son is.

'I'm glad. Eleonora told me, but I wanted to hear it from you,' Cassy began. 'Steve texted me that he was at your place a few minutes before the fire. However, as far as I understand, he was not with you at the time.'

Marta didn't answer right away, and Cassy could hear her quickened breathing. She seemed to be considering what to say to her.

'No, he wasn't with me at the time.'

'And after that?'

'I don't know where Steve is, Cassy. I know he took Charlie, but they're not with me now.'

It didn't escape Cassy's mind that Marta hadn't answered her question. Steve had probably been at her place with the dog right after he left town and then had gone somewhere else. Wherever he was, his mother wasn't going to tell her. *Well okay,* Cassy thought. She would find a way to find her husband.

'I want to let you know that I declared him missing,' she said.

'But why?' protested Marta.

'Because we don't know where he is. And because we don't know where Charlie is either.'

'Cassy, I know it's hard on you, but don't you think it's too much to declare him missing?'

'Marta, do you know something that I don't know?'

'No, honey, I don't know where Steve is. I'm worried too, and I want us to find him.'

'Then please don't stop me from doing my job. We haven't seen or heard from Steve in a few days, and we want to find him as quickly as possible, right?'

'You're right. But I kept thinking you two had a fight about something, and that's why he left town.'

'We didn't fight. He lied to me. He told me he was going to see you. Now it turns out that he didn't think to come to you at all. He probably didn't come to you last month either.'

'No, he didn't come,' admitted the old woman, and Cassy felt nervousness in her voice. It was time to end the conversation. Steve's mother was not to be held responsible for her son's actions.

'Good night, Marta. I'll call you as soon as I know more.'

'Good night,' said the old woman, and Cassy heard her heavy sigh. Marta definitely knew something more, but she wasn't sharing it. Cassy liked her mother-in-law. She felt closer to her sometimes, than to her own mother. Marta was the type of person who would make you tea, put cookies on the table, and listen to anything you had to say without interrupting or reprimanding you. And best of all, without giving you advice and direction on what to do with your life, something Cassy couldn't say about her own mother. Her mother-in-law could often tell by her voice whether she was feeling well or not and always managed to calm her down with just a few words. Today, however, things were different, and their conversation felt as if they were from two different planets. Cassy closed her eyes and thought that in just a few days, she had lost the solid ground beneath her feet. She no longer had a home or a husband. The dog she loved so much was also not with her. Hell, even the clothes and shoes she was wearing weren't hers. The only thing she still had was her job. But she could lose that very quickly if she went against Steve's family. Only now did Cassy realize that she had completely bound herself to his family, and from now on, she had to be very careful. She got up slowly and walked over to Doctor Fisher.

'You can't sleep, huh?' he asked.

'Yes. I won't be getting any sleep soon.' She sat down in the chair next to him. 'Did Eleonora give you the bottle?'

'Yes, but I don't think this is the bottle you drank from this morning. Zlotov said that there are no prints on it, which would be impossible if you had held it in your hand.'

'He didn't mention it to me.'

'You were talking to Burke when he called.'

'Sure. Then someone switched the bottles.'

'Yes, I guess that's exactly what happened.'

Doctor Fisher watched her. She could see sympathy in his eyes. The doctor was a few years younger than Cassy, with blue eyes and brown curly hair that he didn't cut often. He was one of those people who were very diligent in their work but did not care about their appearance.

'How many years ago did you return to live in Balkan?' she asked him.

'Five years ago.'

'Why did you come back?'

Doctor Fisher did not respond immediately. His gaze seemed to drift. Cassy's question clearly took him back to another time and place.

'I needed a change, and the vacancy at the hospital here came just in time.'

Cassy looked away from him. It was as if everyone she knew and trusted were now strangers. They had come to work in Balkan for personal reasons.

'Do you regret your decision?'

'Honestly, I do. I'm even considering leaving the town soon. Everything seems to be fine in this city, but I realized over time that it's like living in a house where you think there are no cockroaches, until you happen to wake up one night, turn on the light, and see them walking around on the floor. Or bedbugs that you don't see and don't know are there, but if you look closely, you will see traces of them.'

Cassy looked away from Doctor Fisher, troubled by what he had told her. She hadn't seen any cockroaches or bedbugs, but she could hear the sound of them moving. Something was happening in this city, but she wasn't sure what yet, and she had sensed it a long time ago. She had simply dismissed the idea that there was something rotten here. She thought she was imagining it, but what Fisher said sobered her up.

'I understand,' she said.

'Do you regret moving?' he asked.

'Until now, I didn't regret it, but now ... I honestly don't know what to think. Did you know that Steve is missing?'

'Is he? No, I didn't know, but that explains why he's not here now.'

'He left town during the fire. He also took our dog.'

Cassy didn't know why she was telling the doctor all this. Probably because she felt weak and helpless.

'I'm sorry,' he said.

'Eleonora is his sister. That's why we moved here.'

'The mayor? Steve is the brother of the mayor of the town, and you are the chief of police...'

Doctor Fisher seemed surprised. Cassy, however, sensed another note in his voice. The doctor seemed troubled by the kinship between her and Eleonora.

'What's wrong?' she asked.

'Nothing. I just didn't know you two were related.'

'I thought you knew she was my sister-in-law. Everyone knows it; I never hid that we were here because of her. And didn't I tell you that the water bottle was in Eleonora's house?'

'Everyone calls her *the mayor*; I didn't know you meant her. Anyway, it doesn't matter,' said Fisher, but his tone had changed. Cassy saw his worry and decided it was best to go back to her bed and try to rest. As she moved, she saw in the reflection of the glass medicine cabinet, Fisher typing a message on his phone. The fact that Cassy was related to the town's mayor clearly worried him. But how could he not know about it? Everyone at the police station knew that Eleonora was Steve's sister. However, perhaps no one else was aware.

Cassy lay in her bed and stared at Fisher's back. She would talk to him again in the morning. She was going to make him tell her why he was so worried. For now, however, it was better to stay in bed.

The next morning, Maggie woke her up. Doctor Fisher had gone home to rest, and Cassy was unable to have a conversation with him. A little after nine, Burke came to pick her up, and they headed to the Archive Warehouse. When they went inside, they saw a cleaner washing the floor, and it was immediately clear to them that the traces they had come to check had already been completely washed away. Cassy and Burke went around the warehouse several times, examined the cabinets from which they thought the documents had been stolen, and after not seeing or finding anything new, they headed to the newly formed police station.

'Do you think someone called the cleaning lady to clean on purpose?' Cassy asked.

'I am certain. Zlotov said that they have closed this part of the Archive Warehouse while the investigation is ongoing. I think someone removed the tape from the door and called the cleaner. She said she promised to go yesterday, but her child got sick and that's why she didn't go until this morning. If we had arrived half an hour earlier, we might have found something.'

Cassy agreed with him.

'What did you want to show me?' she asked him as they walked towards the Sports Centre.

'Not now. Let's meet at three o'clock at Jill's gazebo.'

'Okay,' she agreed and entered the building. Burke, however, did not follow her but turned and continued walking down the still ash-covered street.

Cassy felt like she was swimming in familiar waters the moment she entered the new police station. The noise of ringing phones, running printers, and muffled conversations soothed her. She spoke with her colleagues, then gave a brief report on the thefts and the search for the perpetrators. Finally, she called Zlotov and retreated to the room they had designated as her office. Fortunately, nothing had been lost in the fire at the old office; since Cassy had been in charge of the city's police, all information had been saved online, and physical evidence had been sent to Rila. Cassy was glad she'd made that change then, even though she'd met resistance from the older policemen. Over time, they got used to it, and for a long time, no one protested about it.

'The printout of Steve's phone,' said Zlotov, and handed her some sheets. 'I figured I'd better print them out for you in case you want to pick them up outside the police station. Tomorrow, Michael will bring you the new laptop, and you will be able to check the information yourself.'

Cassy nodded and pushed the sheets aside. She would examine them later in peace.

'Tell me briefly if there is any news.'

'Nothing on Steve. There is no sign of him. None of his friends has heard or seen him. Bobby drove him out of town and left him in Rhodope shortly after the fire. That's the last we know. His phone has also been switched off since that day, and there are no outgoing calls or messages. I haven't looked at the printout; I thought you'd better do that.'

'What else is new? Something about the thieves?'

'Yes. Sarah the Quick confessed to the stolen jewellery. She entered the houses before and after the fire. I think it's good if you talk to her.'

'Why?'

'Sarah spotted someone shortly before she left town on the day of the fire. I urged her to tell me who she saw, but she wants to talk to you about it.'

'Okay, I'll talk to her. And what about the other thefts?'

'Chris won't admit to them, but I have enough evidence to pressure him to talk. I thought I'd visit him in the cell right after we finished here.'

'Great. I'll talk to Sarah the Quick, and you go talk to Chris. Where are they?'

'We locked them in the basement.'

Cassy stood up and, out of habit, reached for her gun. 'Did you find my gun?'

'Your safe is here, but we haven't opened it. I guess your gun is still in there.'

Zlotov showed Cassy her safe and stepped aside. She entered the combination, and the metal door opened. Her weapon and all the documents inside were intact. Cassy took a deep breath and breathed a sigh of relief. Some of the documents in the safe were very important, and she mentally thanked Sylvester, or Sully as everyone called him, who had advised her to get a safe that would withstand a fire. Sully was Eleonora's missing husband. *Where is he now?* Cassy thought. *Is he dead?* She briefly opened his file. Her brother-in-law had disappeared very suddenly, and all efforts by Cassy and her colleagues to find him had failed. It was one of the unsolved cases that she kept in her safe and returned to from time to time. Although everything she knew about the case was in her online police account, sometimes she preferred to read things in print and turn the pages as if she were reading a book. This always helped her focus better on the information. Cassy flipped through Sully's thick file again, but nothing new came to her mind, so she closed the file, then the safe, and slowly made her way down to the basement.

The underground was cool and bright. Until recently, they had used it for other purposes, but now they had divided it into three small parts. There were two cells and a small office equipped with a chair and a small desk. Zlotov was sitting behind the desk, looking at something on his laptop.

'You have to look at this,' he told Cassy.

She moved closer and stood behind him so that she could see the image on the screen better. 'What is this?'

'Traces from the Archive Warehouse. We managed to photograph them two days ago.'

Cassy stared. There was an open filing cabinet in the picture, and grey ash right under the cabinet.

'There is no black soot, only grey ash,' she said.

'What?' asked Zlotov.

'No soot. When we arrived at the Sports Centre, there was black soot on the road. Whoever went inside was there before we went. Maybe during the fire or shortly after.'

'But who would risk his own life?'

'The one who set it on fire, don't you think?' said Cassy and made Zlotov show her all the photos.

'Has Burke seen them?'

'Yes, I showed all the images to him yesterday. I even printed one of them for him.'

That's probably what he wanted to show me yesterday, Cassy thought. Burke had probably noticed that there was no black soot on the floor. She leaned against the wall. The blueprints that were taken from the Archive Warehouse were probably very important to whoever took them. They had to find out right away exactly what was missing from there.

'Interrogate Chris and then go to the Archive Warehouse with Peter. It is very important to know what was taken from there. Let Peter help the employees quickly discover which files are missing.'

'Okay. Sarah the Quick is in the first cell.'

Cassy nodded, took the key Zlotov handed her, and headed for the thief's cell.

Sarah the Quick was a short blonde with thinning hair and teeth darkened by cigarettes. Sarah was approaching fifty, but she never gave up the habit of "unconsciously" taking other people's belongings. The woman had a good sense of humour and self-irony. She wasn't mean and aggressive. On the contrary, over time, Cassy realized that despite her bad habit, Sarah was a good person. She helped her neighbour by babysitting her children when needed. She often shopped for her other neighbour who couldn't walk, and delivered produce to families who couldn't afford better food. Most people in town loved her. Only the people she had robbed passed her by. Sarah the Quick was a strange person, Cassy thought as she entered her cell.

'Sarah, how are you?'

'I am fine. It's cool here, nicer than the old cells.'

'Please, don't tell me you want to extend your stay here because of the coolness?' Cassy laughed.

'No. As much as I'm fine here, and I don't want to go back to the heat up there, I'd rather go home.'

Sarah laughed, then looked at Cassy. She looked her over and shook her head.

'You don't look good, boss. You need rest,' she said.

'I know. I will rest when I find time. I have a lot of work at the moment. Which reminds me to ask you, why do you want to see me?'

Sarah flinched. Her gaze darkened as if she had gone back somewhere in her thoughts. Something was bothering her, Cassy thought as she watched the woman in front of her purse her lips nervously.

'You told Zlotov that you wanted to tell me something important,' Cassy explained, seeing Sarah's concern.

‘That’s right. Can we talk somewhere where no one will hear us?’ Sarah asked.

‘I think so,’ Cassy said, and thought she’d turned the restrooms into an office. She asked Sarah to go to the small room. The woman was very worried; whatever she wanted to say to her was obviously scaring her. Cassy followed, closing the door behind her and leaning against the cool tiled wall.

‘What’s wrong?’ she asked, looking at Sarah. The woman’s hands were shaking slightly. Cassy had never seen her so worried.

‘I saw Sully in one of the houses I was in that day.’

‘Sylvester?’ Cassy was surprised. ‘Are you sure?’

‘I’m sure it was him.’

‘Did he say anything?’

‘No. He didn’t see me. I was hiding under the bed in one of the bedrooms.’

‘How did you know it was him?’

‘I saw him in the mirror. Trust me, I couldn’t believe my eyes. He had a beard, but it was definitely him.’

This time, Cassy started biting her lower lip. Her brother-in-law had made a surprise appearance in town. Or maybe he had never left.

‘What was he doing in the house?’ she asked.

‘He was looking for something in the book section.’

‘Did he find it?’

'I don't know. He moved to the right, and I lost track of him. I don't know what he was looking for, but he stayed in the house for at least three minutes.'

'Which house were you in?'

'Leslie's house.'

'The lawyer?'

'Yes.'

'Isn't Leslie defending you in court?' Cassy asked, seeing Sarah the Quick's guilty look.

'Yes, she is my lawyer.'

'And you robbed her!? Shame on you, Sarah!'

'I didn't take anything from her house. Please don't tell her.'

'This time, you went too far,' Cassy scolded her.

'I know. I'm sorry. Please promise me you won't tell her.'

'Okay, but you promise not to tell anyone about Sully.'

'I promise,' Sarah said, raising her fist high as a sign of an oath. 'When can I leave?'

'I will ask Zlotov. I guess it will take him another day or two to process your paperwork. They are delayed because of...'

'I know, he told me. It's all because of the fire.'

'Yes. And Sarah, thanks for telling me about Sully.'

Cassy walked her out of the small bathroom and locked her back in the cell. What had her brother-in-law been doing in Leslie's house, she wondered as she climbed the steps. If he had been in the house at the time of the fire, he probably lived somewhere near the city. Or in the city itself. Should she tell Eleonora? She had better not tell anyone. Her sister-in-law's insistence on making her drink the poisoned still water had put her on Cassy's list of suspects. Everyone was now a suspect, even Zlotov. Right now, the only person she trusted was Burke.

Cassy went back to her desk, pulled out the printout for Steve's phone calls and messages, and slowly began going through the phone numbers he had called over the past two months. The last two calls were to his sister and his mother, the day after the fire. Cassy felt sick when she saw that. So, Eleonora had lied to her. She had talked to Steve after the fire, so she didn't seem too worried. She was protecting him. But why did Steve need to run and hide? Why didn't he just tell her he wanted a divorce? Cassy's eyes watered. She tried to calm down and look at the facts.

As she looked through the phone numbers, it struck her that her husband had called someone several times almost every day, and the calls were always longer than ten minutes. Cassy punched in the phone number for verification and blinked in surprise when she saw the name. Steve had spoken to Leslie. Several times, the conversations were after midnight. They were lovers, she thought. The truth stunned her. It had all been there, all the signs, but Cassy had ignored them. She stared into the face of the beautiful lawyer. The two of them looked alike. Where they differed was that Cassy would *never* have a relationship with a married man. *Never.*

The realization had just unlocked a helplessness in her that she hadn't felt in years. Cassy squirmed in her chair, trying to hold back the tears. However, what she had experienced in the last few days had taken all her strength, and the realization that her life was not what she had thought it to be broke her down. She held her head in her hands and let her tears just flow. Her colleagues were watching her; two of them tried to approach her and calm her down, but Cassy waved them to stop. She would deal with her feelings on her own. She had done it before, and she would do it again. She looked back at the laptop screen and thought that her only regret was knowing the truth. Sometimes life is better when you're delusional.

-Chapter Seven-

Fish Around

Cassy was focused on the list of missing documents from the Archive Warehouse when Eleonora entered the room.

'I thought you were going to stop by the house this morning,' she said.

'I had work to do.'

'You don't look good, Cassy. You need a break.'

'I will rest more during the weekend. How are the kids?' Cassy asked, trying to change the subject.

'They are fine. They are asking about you. I brought you lunch and clothes to change into.'

'Thanks, but I'm not hungry.'

'Cassy, what's up? You are acting weird.'

'I looked at Steve's phone printout.'

Eleonora blinked. 'Why are you looking at that?'

'I declared him missing yesterday.'

'But why would you do that?' The mayor was surprised. Her confusion was visible.

'Because I don't know where he is.'

'That doesn't mean he's in danger, does it?'

'Aren't you worried? No, don't answer me. I know you're not. You talked to him a few days ago. Where is he, Eleonora? Where's Steve, and where's Charlie?'

Eleonora stared at Cassy but said nothing. Then she got up, straightened her skirt, and prepared to leave.

'If you have any information about where my husband is, you'd better tell me now.'

Eleonora paused, then slowly came back and sat in the chair.

'I don't know where Steve is,' she said, gesturing to Cassy that everyone in the new little police station was listening.

'Then tell me what you know. Why did he leave town?'

'You have to ask him; I don't want to be part of it.'

'I'd ask him, but I don't know where he is. Is he with Leslie?'

The mention of the lawyer seemed to surprise Eleonora. 'Do you know about Leslie?'

'It wasn't hard to guess. He talked to her around the clock.'

'Then ask her where your husband is,' said Eleonora. She got up again and quickly went to the door.

'Don't wait for me for dinner,' Cassy called after her. She couldn't imagine eating or drinking anything her sister-in-law had brought her, so she threw the box of food in the trash.

'What a mess,' said Zlotov, who was sitting on the vacated chair.

'Yes. I just want to scream.'

Zlotov patted her reassuringly on the shoulder. 'You will get over it.'

'That's right. I definitely will.'

'What are you going to do now? Where will you live? I don't think Eleonora will take you in after this scandal.'

'I might check with the hotels to see if they have any rooms available until I find something to rent.'

'They have no available rooms. Most homeowners with houses damaged by the fire are currently there at municipal expense.'

Cassy stumbled. She hadn't thought about where she would stay.

'Why don't you ask Marina. She rented a small house two blocks from here. She might let you use one of the rooms for a while. You two get along, right?'

'Yes, we understand each other. Thanks, Zlotov. I'll call her in a bit to ask if she'll take me in for a few days while I figure out what to do.'

'You're not going to leave the police force, are you?'

'No, not of my own accord.'

'The mayor won't fire you. She needs you right now, and everyone here loves you. If she kicks you out, it will hurt her rating. Try to work things out between you, though. The last thing this town needs is a feud between City Hall and the police.'

Cassy was silent. She had always separated her private life from her work life. Now, however, things were tightly intertwined, and one could topple the other. She needed to find Leslie and talk to her. But before that, she needed a shower and clean clothes. Cassy picked up the bag of clothes her sister-in-law had brought her and headed for the showers at the Sports Centre. Then, she would think about where she would spend the night. Now it was more important to gather strength and help her colleagues catalog all of the thefts, crimes, and evidence from the time of the fire.

Cassy took a shower and refreshed, and now, more relaxed, returned to the documents she was going through. Zlotov and his colleagues had done a good job and had described all the crimes in detail. At the end of the day, they had solved all cases for all complaints and thefts. That left only three open cases.

Steve and Charlie were still being searched for, as was the person who took the documents from the Archive Warehouse. However, the new case was just as strange as the other two, and Cassy had no idea why anyone would want to do it. Someone had broken into the town's fire department. Only Burke's office was ransacked. Cassy called him and asked him to meet her out somewhere, and since she hadn't eaten in a while, they decided to meet at one of the pubs near the temporary police station.

'I guess that's what you wanted us to talk about the other day,' she told him after they sat down at one of the tables at the back of the pub.

'Yes. I took pictures, and I want to show them to you.'

Burke handed Cassy his phone and let her look at the photos.

'What did they take?'

'Old papers from Sully's time.'

'How old?'

'A few months before he disappeared, he was making surprise safety checks on old disused buildings in the area. Three of the buildings were burned down on the day of the fire. There are two more that I checked outside today but didn't see anything suspicious. I will talk to the owner if I can look at them from the inside as well.'

'What's in the documents? Why are they so important?' Cassy asked as she looked at the menu.

'There is nothing significant in these documents, but someone took quite a risk by entering the fire station in broad daylight. You know, there are almost always people there.'

'Can you give me copies of these documents?'

'No. The checks he made were not entered into the system. It wasn't until the other day that I realized Sully had probably left town suddenly and hadn't been able to pick them up.'

'That explains everything,' Cassy muttered to herself.

'What explains everything?' asked Burke in astonishment.

'Sarah the Quick saw Sully at the house of the lawyer Leslie Arnick.'

'At Leslie's house? What was he doing there?'

'He was looking for something in her library.'

'Did you talk to her?'

'No. I wanted to observe her first. I also have a personal motive for talking to her. Steve talked to Leslie every day, sometimes every night. I guess they had an affair.'

'Leslie and Steve?' Burke was surprised.

'Yes. Steve was in town at the time of the fire and took Charlie with him.'

Cassy's voice was shaking. Taking her dog away from her was something she could not forgive her husband for. With that action, Steve had driven a knife deep into her heart.

'I'm sorry to hear that,' said Burke and patted her sympathetically on the shoulder. 'What will you do now?'

'I will try to find a connection between Leslie and Sully. There is something that connects them, but it's not my cheating husband. At least, that's what my intuition tells me. And what will you do?'

'I demanded all the documents for the burned buildings today. I should get them tomorrow. I'm hoping to find something that will give me a clue as to who the arsonist was and why he did it.'

'Well, we have a plan then. The only thing that worries me is that someone is trying to kill us. Do you have any suspects?'

'Not at all, but I think someone thinks you and I saw something during the fire.'

'I think you are right. You mentioned any footprints in one of the houses. Did you go there with Zlotov?'

'No, but I guess you won't be surprised that it turned out to be in Leslie's house.'

'So, she's the connecting link. I must talk to her tomorrow.'

'I can come with you if you want,' offered Burke.

'You know what, it would be best if we both go. I feel very tired, and I might miss something. Also, my judgement of this woman may be clouded by my personal motive.'

'Okay. I'll come and pick you up in the morning. Where are you staying?'

'Marina will put me up for a while.'

'See you tomorrow then,' said Burke, and, after paying the bill, he left.

Cassy looked after him. Burke was short, and his limp made him even shorter, but there was a stability about him that Cassy hadn't seen in many people. The fireman reminded her a lot of Ron. *Let's hope he doesn't suffer his fate*, she thought. Then she went back to the police station, locked the documents in the safe, and slowly walked to the house rented by Marina. A policeman followed behind her a few paces away. Zlotov hadn't removed her guard. And it was for the best. She no longer felt safe in this city.

The next morning, Cassy and Burke visited the lawyer. Leslie was a few years younger than Cassy, but the wrinkles under her eyes were greater. Her eyes were red; her cheeks and her nose also had a red colour. Cassy assumed they were the result of frequent alcohol use.

'The police chief and the fire chief? Did I do something wrong?' The lawyer smiled, and Cassy wanted to stick a knife in her.

'No. But we want to ask you a few questions.'

'What if I don't want to answer your questions?' Leslie said in a drawling voice.

'I don't see why you shouldn't answer,' Cassy said. 'We are looking for missing people.'

'Right? And who is missing?'

'Sully and Steve.'

'Huh. I didn't know they were missing.'

Leslie was defiant and glared at Cassy. Burke stood between the two women, sensing where things would go if he didn't intervene.

'Leslie, you're the last person Steve talked to,' he said.

'How do you know he didn't call someone else?'

'I declared him missing and reviewed his phone calls,' Cassy explained. 'You have talked often in the last few months. Sometimes you talked for hours at night. We both know what that means. I'm not interested in your affair right now, Leslie. What I want to know is if you know where Steve is.'

'You declared your own husband missing,' said Leslie. 'Very convenient for a police chief. If every woman whose husband left her declared him missing, you'd have a lot of work for the police.'

'He hasn't left me. And no one knows where he is.'

'I don't know where he is either. Maybe you should ask his sister and his mother.'

'I asked them. No one has heard or seen him for almost a week.'

Cassy's words seemed to touch Leslie, and a look of worry appeared in her eyes.

'He was with you when the fire started, wasn't he?' Burke asked her.

'Yes,' she admitted. 'He was with me. Then we heard the explosion, and he went to get Charlie from the flat.'

'He went to his mother after the fire. Then all trace of him was lost. When you heard from him, did he tell you where he was?' Cassy asked.

'He told me that they had a fight with Marta and that he would call me when he settled down somewhere. But he never did. I thought he had decided to come back to you.'

Cassy nodded. Something had happened to Steve after he left Marta's house. 'Did he tell you if Charlie was with him?'

'No. He didn't mention it. You will find Steve, won't you?'

'I hope so,' Cassy said.

'And what can you tell us about Sully?' Burke asked.

Leslie seemed troubled by the question. She looked away and took a deep breath.

'Don't tell me that you had an affair with him too,' Cassy said in a raised voice.

'No. We only had a business relationship.'

'What kind of business relationship?' asked Burke.

'He was my client.'

'On what occasion?'

'It was not related to his work, but to his family.'

'With Eleonora?' Cassy was surprised.

'I can't tell you more.'

Burke and Cassy looked at each other. Even if they had insisted, Leslie would hardly have told them more. They had to find out for themselves what the family occasion was.

'Did Steve know about this?'

'No. I haven't mentioned anything to him. It never went to trial anyway because Sully disappeared.'

'And he hasn't contacted you since?' Cassy asked.

'No, he didn't. But even if he had contacted me, I wouldn't have told you.'

'Okay,' Burke said and got up from his chair.

Cassy rose as well, but then sat down and stared at Leslie. 'My marriage to Steve was over a long time ago.'

'That's what he told me too. My relationship with him is not something I am proud of. I would appreciate it if you let me know when you find him.'

'To be honest, I'm surprised that he not only abandoned me but also you. This is not typical of Steve. He is caring at heart. I'll call you if I have any new information on him.'

Leslie nodded, and Cassy caught sight of the tears that were falling from the lawyer's eyes. She obviously wasn't indifferent to Steve, she thought and wondered why she didn't have those feelings. Shouldn't she, as his wife, shed tears for him?

Burke patted her shoulder sympathetically. 'Big mess, huh?'

'Yes. She loves Steve, and she is really worried about him. We have to keep looking for him.'

'I'll dig more around Sully's life,' Burke said. 'There is something about his disappearance that is very strange.'

'What do your colleagues say?'

'They speak with respect about him.'

'Do they suspect anything?'

'No. The only thing everyone agrees on is that he has something to do with the fire.'

'You think he set the fires?'

'It is possible. As I told you before, this was a controlled fire. Not many people I know can do that. The aim was that only the administrative buildings in the centre would suffer, and the houses around them. The two gas pipelines had been shut down shortly before, and this stopped the flow of gas to the rest of the town. I now know how it was done, but I don't know who and what motive he would have.'

'I am wondering the same thing. I think Eleonora knows more than she's letting on, but I can't ask her.'

Burke watched her as if trying to figure out something.

'That's it,' said Cassy. 'That's why you looked at me so suspiciously and didn't tell me anything. You think Eleonora and I are close.'

'Aren't you?'

'Yes, you could say we are close. But she never talked to me about Sully. All I know about him is from Steve and Marta.'

'Maybe you know more than you think, and that's why someone tried to poison you.'

'Maybe,' Cassy said thoughtfully. 'Eleonora was definitely hiding something, but what? And was it related to Sully, or was it something else?'

'Try to talk to her,' Burke advised. 'Maybe it has nothing to do with Sully or the town.'

'I will call her today, but I doubt she will agree to talk to me. Not after our fight yesterday.'

Burke and Cassy walked slowly down the sidewalk, and when they reached the new police department, they saw a commotion outside the door. Zlotov was arguing with someone, and his face was red. Cassy had never seen him like this.

'Zlotov, what's going on?' she asked.

The young man turned to Cassy and, on seeing her, his mouth fell open.

'Cassandra Silver, from this moment, you are removed from office. You are no longer the chief of police,' a white-haired middle-aged man answered instead.

Cassy, like Zlotov, opened her mouth to say something, but the shock of what the man had said left her speechless.

'What is the exact reason you are removing her?' Burke asked.

'I can't say that. Only the mayor of the city can give you details.'

Cassy and Burke looked at each other. Eleonora had removed her sister-in-law. The question was whether she had done the same with him.

'Can I get my things?' Cassy asked.

'Yes. You must also hand over to me all the documents in the cases you are handling, as well as your phone and weapon.'

'Would you introduce yourself?' Burke asked.

'Chief Bordeaux. I'm the new chief of police,' the man said, making room for Burke and Cassy to enter the office. Cassy looked around. Her colleagues stood around her shocked, obviously as amazed as she was at what was happening. Something had caused Eleonora to fire Cassy, but what, she wondered. It took her about an hour to convey the necessary information to Bordeaux. Cassy then took the few belongings she had and walked out into the street, still in shock.

'Come,' Burke told her and led her to the fire station. He needed to know if a replacement had been sent for him as well.

'Everything is calm, Burke,' said one of his colleagues when he saw them enter.

'Come into my office,' Burke suggested to Cassy. 'I will make a coffee, then we can talk.'

'Okay,' she muttered. She still couldn't believe what had happened. Why did Eleonora appoint a new police chief? And what exactly was going on in this town?

'Only you were removed,' said Burke, carrying two cups of coffee. 'Everyone else has kept their positions.'

'So, it's personal,' Cassy whispered.

'Think, what have you done? Why is she removing you?'

'Because of Steve. Everything was fine until I reported Steve missing.'

'But why? He's her brother, isn't he?'

'Exactly. Why would she do that?' Cassy wondered.

'Why don't you go home and rest?' Burke advised her. 'You are tired. I'll ask around and come back tonight to tell you what I learn.'

Cassy agreed. She drank the coffee he brought her and headed to Marina's house. A bad surprise awaited her there too.

'You can't stay with me,' Marina told her. The old woman's hands trembled as she spoke. Someone had threatened her, Cassy thought, and without protest, she left the house as quickly as possible. All this meant one thing: Her sister-in-law was chasing her out of town. Whatever hive Cassy had unwittingly reached into had been disturbed, and now the bees chased and stung her. Left on the street, she realized she had to leave the town as quickly as possible to avoid hurting other people close to her. She returned to the fire station.

'Burke, you have to take me to the capital.'

'Why? What's happening?'

'Whatever is happening in this town is bigger than my husband's disappearance. I have to get out of here, or they'll start hurting the people I'm talking to.'

'Who are *they*? And why are they keeping me on?' asked Burke and immediately answered the question himself. 'They need me for something.'

'I think so too. You probably have something they need. I advise you to pack your things and go to your family.'

'And what will you do?'

'I will continue the search for Steve and Sully.'

'How will you do that? You don't work for the police anymore.'

'Don't worry about it. I already have a plan. Just take me to Rila. I will be waiting for you outside Clay's house.'

'Okay,' Burke agreed. 'I'm going to get the car.'

At that moment, Zlotov stood next to them.

'Boss, you forgot your book.'

The young man handed Cassy a book, and before she could protest that it wasn't hers, Zlotov turned the first corner and disappeared from her sight. Cassy looked at Burke, then at the book, and when she read the book's title, she was speechless.

'Run,' she shouted to Burke.

He looked at her in astonishment.

'Run! They are coming for us,' she said and forced him to run in the opposite direction of the fire station.

As she ran, Cassy pulled her personal phone out of her pocket and tossed it into the first trash can she saw. Then she gestured for Burke to do the same. At noon, the streets of Balkan were usually lively, but on this day, the town seemed to have died down. Cassy could feel people's eyes on her, but she couldn't see who was watching her.

'We have to hide somewhere,' she said to the fireman.

'Where?' he asked.

'Which buildings in the upper part of the town are deserted?'

'There are two in three blocks.'

'We're going there. Run, we don't have much time!' she shouted and pushed him forward. Burke didn't protest this time but ran as fast as he could. The two buildings were practically glued together. One was an abandoned factory, and the other was an unfinished kindergarten. Burke hesitated for a second over where to enter but then pushed through the iron fence of the factory and pulled Cassy behind a large, rusted billboard.

'What's happening?' he asked after his breathing calmed down.

Cassy said nothing; she seemed to freeze for a moment, then she listened. The sound Burke also heard was familiar. They had launched drones after them. But why? The large iron billboard behind which they were hiding had broken in two, and Cassy crawled into the middle. Burke followed her. The sound of the drone could still be heard nearby. They both cowered and covered their faces with their hands. This kind of drone detected the glare from people's teeth and eyes. Cassy heard more drones approaching. The drones circled for another minute or two, then moved away.

'Shit,' Burke uttered. 'Why are they looking for us?'

'I can only guess,' Cassy said.

'And what is your guess?'

'I think they want to arrest us.'

'On what charge?'

'I don't know.'

They remained hidden in the billboard. The weather was warm, but after half an hour, they heard thunder. Cassy wasn't sure whether she was happy about the rain or not. Now, she had to come up with a plan to get to Rila as quickly as possible.

'What's in the factory?' she asked, glancing away from the billboard briefly to try to gauge how good their cover was.

'Old machines. Some of them are coated with machine oil, and I've been looking for the owner to remove them. Engine oil is flammable and ... I don't know why I'm telling you all this.'

'Can we hide inside temporarily?'

'Not for long. If someone decides to go inside and check if we're there, they'll find us quickly.'

'Okay, and what's in the other building?'

'There is nothing there, and they will find us even faster.'

Cassy looked back at the old factory. They didn't have much of a choice. They had to go inside; they couldn't stay curled up in the billboard forever.

'What time is it?' she asked.

Burke looked at his watch, and they both cried out in fright. His smartwatch had led the drones to the factory. Burke quickly removed it from his hand and flung it as far away as possible.

'I hope that the person who is chasing us decided that you threw it away before we came.'

'I hope so too,' said the fireman and began to swear, something he only seemed to do at times like this.

They decided to stay hidden in the billboard for a while longer. A few minutes later, the drones appeared again, this time accompanied by two men.

'Where did they disappear?' asked the one man. 'I'm sure they turned this way.'

'They hid somewhere.'

The men stood in front of the billboard but did not look inside; instead, they continued towards the factory.

'It's locked,' said one.

'They may have entered somehow.'

The two men walked around the building, but all the windows were tightly sealed.

'There's no way they got inside. They are somewhere else.'

At that moment, Burke's watch beeped, and the men headed towards it.

'He threw away his smartwatch. They're probably not here. Let's check the other building,' said the older of the two and left the factory area. Cassy and Burke breathed a sigh of relief as they saw them walk away.

'They almost found us,' said Burke. Then he turned to Cassy. 'What was in the book?'

'Nothing. However, it was the title that tipped me off. A kind of code, a warning from a colleague.'

'So Zlotov warned you in time.'

'Someone sent him to warn me. Zlotov does not know about this code.'

'Who then?' Burke was surprised.

'We must go to Rila immediately. What is happening here, in my opinion, is not only local. It is bigger than I thought, but I'll know the details when I get to Rila.'

'Cassy, who warned you?' Burke asked again.

She hesitated before answering him. 'My former intelligence chief.'

'Ronald Adrian Nan?'

'Yes, Ronald Adrian Nan, but everyone calls him RAN. How do you know about him?'

'He was also my boss for a while.'

The two looked at each other.

'How did he find out about what was happening here?' she wondered.

'The fire in Balkan is all over the media. RAN must have seen it.'

'Well, you're right. I guess everyone wants to know how the fire started. There's no way the Intelligence Agency didn't know about it.'

'Now at least I am calm that my family will be fine.'

'Yes, RAN will take care of Berta and the children. But where is my family? Where are Steve and Charlie?' Cassy wondered. 'We need to get to Rila as quickly as possible.'

'I don't think we will be able to get out of here in one piece anytime soon. Better wait until dark. I think they put someone to watch the road to the capital. Better to stay here for now.'

Cassy agreed with him. Their cover was uncomfortable, but she felt secure in it.

'They will continue to search for us for hours,' she said. 'Better prepare for a long wait. What time was it when I looked at the watch?'

'Half-past four.'

'So, we have to stay here for at least six hours. After dark, we'll decide where to go.'

'What if we go to Sam's lodge again?' Burke suggested.

'I often went to the lodge with Charlie, and I am convinced that they will look for us there.'

'They're unlikely to search the mountains at night. Do you trust the lodge host?'

'I think so.'

'So, we'll go there.'

'I don't know, Burke. I don't want to involve other people in this.'

'Do you have another plan, Cassy? Do you know someone else with access to a phone and a car that's far enough out of town?'

'No,' she admitted.

'So, you don't have a plan B?' he asked, looking her straight in the eyes.

'No, I don't have a plan B.'

'Then we have to go to the lodge.'

Cassy agreed. Burke was right; Sam was their only chance to leave the area. No one else in the town would help them. The frightened looks she saw from the people through the windows proved it. People were in a panic. First the fire, now this. They had probably been told that she and Burke were to blame for setting fire to the town, and anyone would have believed it. In the end, everyone had done their best to get away from the burning city, and only the two of them had been left behind. It even sounded suspicious to Cassy when she thought about it.

'What if Sam decides to betray us?' Doubts began to take over her little by little.

'And who will he call in the forest? Even if he calls someone, it will take time for them to arrive.'

'You're right,' she said and sighed. They had no other choice; the lodge was the best escape option for now. If they stayed in town, someone would see them and call the police. *What a mess*, Cassy thought.

'How long do you think it will take us to reach the lodge?' Burke asked.

'We will have to climb for a long time. Since it will be dark and we will have to be very careful not to be sees, it will take us much longer to reach the lodge than usual. If we leave at ten o'clock, we'll probably be there by four or five in the morning.'

'Okay. Let's try to sleep until then,' Burke said, and he tried to stretch his legs. However, the cramped space beneath the billboard did not allow this comfort. Burke sighed heavily, leaned his head back, and closed his eyes. Cassy tried to do the same, but she couldn't stop thinking about the events of the day. How had RAN known about what was going on in the town and that she was in trouble? It had all started with Steve being reported missing. His being searched for had obviously affected someone's interests. Her intuition told her that her husband would not just run away. Cassy's heart began to beat fast with worry. *What had people in this town gotten themselves into?* she wondered.

-Chapter Eight-

Mist

Cassy dreamed that it was raining. She could even smell the rain. She felt cool and took a deep breath. Then something fell on her hair and, half-asleep, she reached out to find out what it was. Her hand touched the cold iron frame, and it woke her up. Cassy realized that she and Burke were still beneath the large, iron billboard. She looked at the sleeping fireman. His forehead was sweaty, and his lips were tightly pursed. Whatever he was dreaming about wasn't something that made him happy, Cassy thought, and she looked up. The sky had darkened, and it was drizzling for the first time in months. The rain made her smile.

The raindrops woke Burke up too. He looked around in confusion until he met her gaze.

'It's raining.' He smiled too.

'Yes. I had forgotten how good it felt to feel the raindrops running down my face. The rain will clear the air in the town.'

'That's right, but if the night isn't clear, it will take us longer to get to the lodge,' said Burke.

'I know a direct path. I often used to pass by there with Charlie. We'll have to leave soon, though, to get to the path before dark. Do you have a flashlight?'

'Yes.' Burke was still in his fireman's uniform. He reached into one of the pockets and pulled out a small flashlight. He tested it and put it back in his pocket.

Cassy looked up again. The rain and clouds would be their cover as they climbed the mountain, but by the time they got there, there would be nothing to hide them. They had to cross at least two lamp-lit streets to reach the Mountain Path. They could have gone around the perimeter of the town, but that would have put them at even greater risk of being seen. They needed cover. She looked around and saw a large pile of iron bars. Some of them were covered with a lot of rust.

'Come,' she said to Burke and headed for the pile. He followed her. Cassy took one of the iron bars and began rubbing her clothes with it. Her jeans quickly soaked up the rust and turned a rusty orange where the rod had rested. Burke quickly picked up on her idea and also rubbed his uniform with the rod. After the fire, there were many new workers in the town from other localities who had come to help clear the remains of the destroyed buildings. Most collected the foundations and concrete in trailers, but there were some on the streets that they carried for scrap iron and other metal things they could sell. Cassy wanted her and Burke to look like those workers. She tousled her hair and let it fall forward to cover her face. The rain helped her look unkempt and wretched. Burke, in turn, found some soot that was now wet and had Cassy put some on his face. Then, they also rubbed soot on their clothes. Finally, they looked at each other.

'You don't look like yourself.' She smiled at Burke after examining him from head to toe.

'You don't look like yourself either. It would be better if we took some iron bars with us.'

They chose some lighter iron bars and slowly made their way out of the abandoned factory. With bowed heads, they entered the street and, without speaking, continued forward. Cassy's heart was racing – the two rods she had taken were heavy in her hands, but she was doing her best to hold them. She was definitely not in her best shape; the time she had given herself to recover was not enough. She needed at least two more weeks of rehab, she thought, but she was unlikely to be able to take that long off.

She looked around and saw that they had almost reached the Mountain Path. Two women passed them in a hurry to hide from the rain. No one paid them any attention, and she and Burke successfully entered the forest. The moment she felt safe, Cassy threw away the iron bars and sat on the ground. Burke also sat down next to her.

'I need a minute or two of rest,' she told him.

The rain had increased, and they could both hear the drops falling on the leaves of the trees. It somehow calmed them down. After the short rest, Cassy and Burke began to climb up, illuminating the way with the small flashlight. They could hear their own footsteps. Sometimes one of them would step on a dry branch or a pile of dry leaves, and the sound was so clear that it made them stop and look around. The forest was dark, as if made only of shadows. The air was heavy with heat from the earth and moisture from the rain. From time to time, they heard the screeching of birds and the howling of unknown animals. Cassy's skin crawled every time she heard those sounds.

'It's an owl. Melody, my little daughter, was studying the animals that live on this mountain and their sounds,' Burke said.

'I hope you're right, and it's an owl. That sound will definitely haunt me in my dreams.'

They continued climbing the path until Cassy got tired. 'I have to rest. I think we're halfway there. After climbing this hill, we will have to descend again and follow the main trail to the lodge.'

Burke sat down next to her.

'Cassy, what do you think they think we know? Why are they chasing us?'

'I don't know, but it must be because of something from the time of the fire.'

'Why do you think so?' Burke was leaning against a tree and taking everything out of his pockets as he talked to her.

'Because someone tried to suffocate me with a pillow shortly after, then someone shot at you and tried to poison me. However, no matter how hard I try, I can't remember anything strange from around that time.'

'Maybe we didn't see anything, but whoever wants us dead doesn't know about it,' he suggested and handed her a candy from the Halls's packet he had taken out of one of his pockets. Cassy gratefully accepted the candy; she needed something to cheer her up.

'Something tells me that we have seen something very important, but we do not realize what it is yet,' she said, and she leaned against the tree next to him. 'I only remember the pain in my ankles.'

'And I only remember the pain, but there is definitely something that is gnawing at me. We saw something then, Cassy. We just have to remember what.'

'Maybe it will happen at some point.'

Cassy stood up, signalling to Burke that they should go. They walked for a long time in silence, listening for unusual sounds. The rain gradually stopped, and so did the screech of the owl. However, the movement of animals could still be felt around them. The rain made the forest feel more alive than ever, Cassy thought. It was as if every creature had come out to enjoy the coolness. Cassy and Burke walked with tired steps. Shortly before reaching the main trail to the lodge, they stopped to rest again. She looked up at the sky. The clouds had gone, and in their place, the moon was visible. Its light illuminated everything around them.

'We'd better not use the flashlight from now on. The path will be wide, and I don't think we will get lost,' she said.

Burke was about to agree, but at that moment, they heard male voices close by.

'It was a waste of time to come here,' said one of them.

'Yes. Most likely, they have already left the area,' agreed the other one.

Cassy recognized the voices of the two men who had followed them to the abandoned factory. The men were walking straight towards Cassy and Burke, but at the last moment, they turned and continued on the other path that led to the lower part of Balkan. Cassy and Burke didn't dare move until they were sure the two men were far enough away.

'It's good that we stopped to rest,' said Cassy.

'Yes. At least now we know no one will be looking for us here. Or at least not tonight.'

Burke got up and looked around. The clouds had reappeared, and he shone his flashlight to see where they were going.

'Maybe tonight the moon will not help us, and we will have to light our way up.'

'Let's hope there are no other people looking for us,' Cassy said quietly. They walked up the steep path, each lost in thought. It was a long walk to the lodge. The drive up was almost two hours, and the walk seemed like an eternity to Cassy. They had to stop to rest in two more places. The temperatures were dropping lower every minute.

'I can't believe I'm saying this, but I'm dying of a cold. I had forgotten how cold it is up in the mountains.'

'I feel cold too. We're tired and wet, Cassy. It's normal to feel that way.'

'I can't wait to get to the lodge,' she said, remembering the nice warm tea with which Sam often welcomed her in the winter.

When they arrived, they saw that there was light in the lodge. Sam was out on the porch, shining a large lantern in front. When he saw them, he waved at them.

'I was expecting you,' he said and gestured for them to come inside.

'How did you know we were coming?' Cassy asked him.

'I heard that both the entry and exit roads to Balkan are closed, and I assumed that you would come here and seek help. Come in; you must be tired and hungry.'

'Thank you,' said Burke, but he didn't step inside and began to look around nervously as if expecting someone else to appear.

'There's a newlywed couple in the room upstairs, but I don't expect any trouble from them,' said Sam.

'Excuse me, but I find your welcome strange. Who told you we were coming?' Burke asked him.

'Nobody. As I already told you, there are only two exits to get out of the town, and they are blocked. I guessed that you would either hide somewhere in the city itself or wait until dark and come here.'

'Aren't you an ex-cop?' Cassy asked.

'Something like that.'

'Where have you worked before?'

'Everywhere. I'll tell you my life story one day. Now, sit down to eat and rest. I don't think you have much time. Two men called here looking for you. I imagine they will come back looking for you here again. They said that if they don't find you by morning, they will use drones to look for you in the mountains. No wonder they came here at dawn.'

'And you want to help us? Why?' Burke shook his head in disbelief.

Sam started in their direction, but Cassy and Burke took a step back, and he stopped.

'I'll tell you later. Come inside now and relax. You are safe, at least for now.'

Cassy and Burke looked at each other. They didn't know whether to trust Sam, and they stood still for a while.

'Okay,' Cassy finally said, still shivering from the cold, 'but first, I'd like to use your phone.'

'I left you a brand-new smartphone in the cupboard upstairs. You can use it; you just have to activate the SIM card. Before you go, tell me if you have any news about Steve.'

'No one knows where he is, not even Marta,' she said and went upstairs to the room where she usually stayed. The moment she entered, her memories hit her. She had spent many good times here with her dog. Sometimes Steve came with them too. This lodge was her refuge from stress, and Cassy had always felt good here. Long walks in the woods and breaks by the stream soothed her. However, she hadn't come on vacation now, she remembered, and went to the bedside table, turned on the phone left there, and called RAN.

'You saved yourself, then,' said her former boss.

'Yes. How did you know we were in danger?'

'*You* were in danger; Burke should have stayed there.'

'Really?' She was surprised.

'Yes. They just put him on the wanted list. But it's better that he comes with you.'

'RAN, I have no idea why these people are chasing me and why they want to kill me. Do you know something? Who are they?'

'No, I know nothing, and that's the strange thing. Usually, we get some advance information that something somewhere is going to happen, but not in this case.'

'How did you know I was in danger then?'

'Marina and I have been friends since before you were born. It was pure coincidence that you moved to the town she lived in and that you lived on the same block. I asked her to watch over you.'

'But why?'

'I told you before you married Steve that there were gaps in his record. Unfortunately, I still don't know what happened to him at that period in time, but my intuition told me that I should protect you.'

'Thanks!' Cassy whispered. 'Now what's next? Can you find us a car to come with Burke to Rila?'

'Don't come to Rila. Stay in Balkan.'

'But how ... why?' Cassy was confused. For her, returning to the town would only bring her trouble. However, RAN clearly did not think so.

'I will send someone tonight to the lodge with all the documents and files we have on the people in Balkan. Stay there temporarily and go over all the information with Burke.'

'But ...'

'Cassy, don't worry. Everything will be fine. I need two days to prepare your new contracts, but from now on, you and Burke will work for me.'

'You mean for the Intelligence Agency?'

'Yes, I mean for the Intelligence Agency. No one can arrest you because you will be under our protection. But I want you to listen carefully. Something is going on in this town, and we need to find out what it is. Between you and Burke, you know most of the people there. Focus, and you will find what's going on.'

'You should talk to Burke. He's worried about his family.'

'They are with us. Berta is, of course, furious, but she'll get over it.'

'Okay, I'll tell him to call you in a little while.'

'Rest for a few hours and call me when you receive the package.'

'Who will bring it?' Cassy asked.

'A little bird will come,' said RAN and laughed.

After she finished talking to RAN, Cassy joined the men in the living room and gave the phone to Burke to talk to their boss. She let him talk and moved into the kitchen with Sam.

'How long have you known RAN?' she asked him.

'Did he tell you that we know each other?'

'No, but if he has ordered us to stay here, then he knows who you are. He wouldn't risk his action failing by leaving us with someone he didn't know well.'

Sam was making tea, with his back to Cassy. She expected him to say something, but he didn't. He didn't turn to talk to her. Instead, he opened the fridge, took out a few items, and started making sandwiches.

'I guess you are hungry,' he said finally.

'You avoid answering my questions. How can I trust you if I don't know what you're up to?'

'I guess you just have to listen to your intuition and trust me. You are safe here, and you know it.'

'But I don't know who you really are.'

Cassy took the cup of tea he handed her and sat down at the large kitchen table. Burke, who had finished talking to RAN, also joined them.

'RAN and I have known each other for many years, but I can't tell you how we met. Even if I did, you would hardly believe me. In my opinion, you have two choices: trust me and stay here for a while or leave.'

'We'll stay here,' Cassy said. 'Since RAN trusts you, I will too.'

'Good decision,' he muttered and handed her a plate of food. 'Now eat.'

Cassy looked at the sandwiches Sam had made. She was hungry, but she didn't reach out to take one. Burke was also hesitant.

'I won't poison you,' said the lodge host. He took a bite from one of the sandwiches and began to chew, looking Cassy and Burke in the eyes. After swallowing the food, he pushed the plate of sandwiches towards them again, and this time they each took one.

'I am not your enemy. On the contrary, I, like you, want to know what is happening in Balkan, and I will help you as much as I can. If I wanted to kill you, I would have done it by now.'

Cassy agreed. Sam was right, there had been plenty of time for him to hurt them one way or another. And if RAN trusted him, so would she, even though this secrecy made her nervous.

After eating, they all moved to the larger dining room and rested on two comfortable sofas, waiting for the courier to arrive with the documents. Cassy lay back and tried to sleep, but she couldn't. She had wrapped herself in two blankets but was still shivering from the cold. The sofa she was lying on was right in front of the fireplace that Sam had lit. She and her dog had spent many hours here, and now the memories came flooding back to her, one after the other. It was as though Charlie and Steve were staring at her. She missed the routine they had created for themselves. Now, sitting here on the sofa in front of the fire, she felt abandoned and lonely, vulnerable to the unknown. Cassy wasn't worried about her life. Her profession was risky, and she had prepared for death for years, but she didn't want to go like that without knowing what was going on around her. Before, when she risked her life, she knew who the enemy was; she knew what the mission was. But now everything was dark and hidden. She felt like she was walking in a mist.

'Why are you not sleeping?' Sam asked her. He had gone over to put more wood in the fireplace.

'There are too many questions in my head. Why don't you rest?'

'I haven't been able to sleep at night for a long time,' he said, taking one of the nearby chairs and sitting next to her. 'I haven't slept well in over ten years.'

'Why? What's wrong?'

'The unknown. Like you, I have many questions that I am looking for answers to.'

'I thought that lodge hosts were people with peace of mind and tranquillity.'

'The other lodge hosts, maybe. My life's mission is not over yet.'

'How many years have you owned the lodge?'

'Six years,' he answered and sighed a little.

So, he had moved two years before she accepted the job.

'So, you know the previous mayor?'

'No. I moved here shortly after Eleonora won the election.'

'I've always wondered how, in just one year, she managed to win the trust of the people in the town and win the mayoral election,' said Cassy as she stared at the fire.

'It's a mystery to me too. Have you ever talked to her about it?'

'Yes, several times. She said she just got lucky. The former mayor was caught in theft or corruption.'

'In corruption, but it was never proven. There are still people in town who support him and who think Eleonora planted the evidence back then.'

'But why?'

'I can't tell you that either. Maybe you and Burke should check out that trail as well.'

'Do you know she fired me today?'

'Really? No, I didn't know that. Rumour has it that someone in the capital wants to arrest you, but I didn't know that Eleonora fired you.'

'I think because I reported Steve missing. She was very angry with me. I wonder if she knows where he is and is covering it up.'

'They are very different, aren't they? Steve is moderate and unambitious, or so I thought until recently. Eleonora is his opposite.'

'That's right,' Cassy agreed, resting her head on the pillow. Talking to Sam had worn her out. She stared at the flames and then fell asleep.

-Chapter Nine-

Circle of Life

Cassy dreamed that she was back in the burning building, trying to save Charlie from the flames. The dog barked. She wanted to approach him, but every time she took a step or reached out, the flames licked her skin. Charlie's barks became weaker and weaker. Tears fell from Cassy's eyes; she was crying and screaming at the same time.

'Cassy! Cassy!' Sam was shaking her, trying to wake her up.

She opened her eyes and screamed as she saw his hands wrap around her shoulders.

'Relax. You are having a nightmare. Everything is fine,' he said. She relaxed, and at that moment, she saw that Burke was also next to her.

'Everything is fine,' he told her. 'You probably associated the fireplace flames with the fire. I had a nightmare too.'

Cassy nodded and tried to take a deep breath. Her heart was still racing, and her hands were shaking. She pursed her lips and inhaled through her nose this time. Sam was seated on her right, and Burke on her left. They were trying to calm her down. When he was sure she was breathing more calmly, Sam got up and brought her a glass of water.

'Do you feel better?'

'Yes,' she said and took a sip of the cold water.

There was the sound of footsteps from the porch, and the two men rose cautiously. Sam looked out the window, then opened the door. Zlotov entered the lodge wet and tired.

'So, you're the little birdie?' Cassy smiled when she saw him.

'What little bird?' asked Burke and Zlotov at the same time.

'RAN said that a little bird would bring us all the documents.'

'He chose quite a large bird,' said Sam.

'Let me see what you have brought for us.'

Zlotov put the box he was carrying on the table. Burke and Cassy joined him, but Sam retreated to the kitchen. Inside the box were many folders and two laptops.

'I managed to get your laptop before the other people came to the police station.'

'Who came, Zlotov? Who is looking for us?' Cassy asked.

'I thought you knew. They introduced themselves under the name of some agency I had never heard of.'

'How many people are there, and do you know their names?' Burke asked.

'Three people came to the office after you left, but they were constantly talking to someone on the phone, so there are probably four. They introduced themselves as Inspectors Planchet, Athos, and Aramis.'

Sam's laughter filled the room.

'What's funny?' asked Zlotov.

'Their names are not real,' Sam said.

'How do you know that?' Burke was surprised.

'They are characters from *The Three Musketeers* by Alexandre Dumas.'

'Are you sure?'

'I am certain. You can check on the internet if you don't believe me.'

'I'll do it later. Now I have to go back,' said Zlotov, and he sighed heavily. The climb to the lodge with the heavy box had tired him.

'Thanks!' Cassy said, and she sent the young man to the door. 'Be careful.'

'I will be, boss,' he promised, and he sank into the darkness of the forest.

'Whoever these people are, they don't mean us well,' Cassy said quietly, approaching Burke. The two of them took all the folders and started reading the information inside.

A few hours later, the newlyweds had left, and Burke and Cassy had turned the living room into an office. Sam had found them a board on which they pinned the pictures of the people they were interested in. Also, near the board, they stacked four piles of papers.

'Let's summarize,' said Cassy. 'We have six burned buildings, eight missing blueprints of abandoned buildings from the Archive Warehouse, and two missing men in the last two years. Both are close to my sister-in-law, the mayor, Eleonora Bulbur. We also have a former mayor accused of corruption, for which no one has any proof. Let's not forget the former police chief, who left town in a hurry. Anything else?'

'We were both new to town, and we were given the two vacant positions. I think Eleonora must be at the heart of it all, and we are part of her plan. The question is, *what the hell is going on?* Was she connected to some criminal business, and did it under our noses?' Burke looked at Cassy as he spoke.

She stared at the board, which was now covered with photos and documents.

'But how?' she asked, looking away from the documents. 'I spent a lot of time with Eleonora. Nothing has suggested to me that she has a side business or that she has a needle with someone.'

'But the disappearance of her husband and her brother is strange. Sully's appearance during the fire is also questionable.'

Sam was surprised. 'Is Sully in Balkan?'

'Yes. One of our known criminal contacts saw him.'

'But why is he hiding?'

'That's what I've been asking myself,' said Cassy, and she sat thoughtfully on the chair. 'Sully and Eleonora seemed to be in love and looked happy. Then he disappeared. But to be honest, after his disappearance, Eleonora didn't talk much about him, and that puzzled me at times. She didn't even ask me if I had any news about him. Now that I think about it, it was almost as though she knew where he was. I questioned her for hours, questioned Sully's friends and colleagues, hoping to find some information that would lead me to him, but he seemed to have evaporated.'

'Strange behaviour for a woman in love,' Burke said. 'If I disappeared, Berta would turn the world upside down looking for me and would stand in front of your office day and night.'

'You know you got lucky with her, right?' Sam said.

'Of course, I know.' Burke smiled. 'Short and hot, that's the first thing I thought of her when I met her. And you know what the first thing I got from her was? A loud, resounding slap.'

Sam and Cassy laughed.

'And what earned you the slap?' asked the lodge host.

'I told her she was short and hot.'

'Burke.' Cassy laughed. 'You just added fuel to the fire.'

'Yes, but it had an effect. Now I am married to her.' The fireman smiled contentedly. 'I don't want to know how RAN will deal with her questions. She must have already driven him crazy.'

Burke looked out the window, still smiling. Cassy watched him for a while, then she picked up the laptop and began searching for information on her sister-in-law.

Just before noon, Sam's dog, Buggy, barked and ran off into the woods.

'A stranger is coming,' Sam said and went out on the porch. Cassy and Burke stayed inside and watched intently from the windows to see who would show up.

'It could have been a squirrel,' Burke said.

'This dog lives among squirrels. No, it's not an animal, it's a human.'

Sam started calling the dog's name, and he finally appeared. A young man Cassy knew was walking behind him.

'Mike,' she whispered softly.

'Who is he?'

'I have seen him at the Sports Centre; he often trains there with my nephew. But what is he doing here now?' Cassy watched as Sam walked to meet the young man. The two of them shook hands and started talking to each other.

'Do you trust Sam?' Burke asked her quietly.

'Yes, I trust him. But Mike coming here is no accident. Someone sent him.'

Sam seemed to sense their eyes on him, and he turned briefly, then he hid his hand behind his waist and signalled to them that everything was fine. Cassy breathed a sigh of relief and backed away from the window. It wasn't long before Sam returned, and Mike started back down the path.

'Marina sent him,' he said after entering the lodge. 'The police department and the fire department have new chiefs. There are also new people in town posing as internal affairs police inspectors. They have created a small office in one of the houses in the town. However, what worries Marina, and the reason why she sent Mike, is that Zlotov did not come home last night. I told Mike he had a long journey from here, and maybe he didn't have time to come home and just went to work.'

'Does she know we're still here?'

'Hardly. I don't think RAN told her, and Zlotov will keep quiet. The boy wanted to know if he had come this far by accident. But why didn't Marina just call to ask me?' Sam wondered.

'With everything going on in the town, she probably didn't want to take a chance and call, in case Zlotov had gone into hiding and sought refuge here,' suggested Cassy. 'I'm worried about him. There is one way to tell if he is at work. We'll call his girlfriend at the hospital and ask her. She's a nurse, and they're unlikely to track calls there.'

'I prefer not to take any chances until RAN tells us. Better call him now,' Sam suggested.

Cassy agreed and immediately dialled her boss's phone number. RAN also did not know if Zlotov had returned to Balkan.

'We will call his girlfriend,' said Cassy, and dialled the number of the temporary hospital. To her surprise, Doctor Fisher picked up the phone.

'Maggie isn't at work today,' he said.

'Okay, thanks,' Cassy said and quickly hung up the phone. Fisher knew her well and could recognize her voice. She didn't want to get him involved.

'What do we do now?' Burke asked.

'We will wait,' Cassy said and opened the laptop. This time, she looked for the local news website, but there was nothing there either. Then she looked for information about Steve and Eleonora's father. Cassy knew from Marta that their father had left them when they were kids, but she had never mentioned his name. Steve and Eleonora didn't talk about him either. They didn't say anything, good or bad, about their dad, which Cassy found strange. She went through their police records, looked for information on the father's name, but the name seemed to have been deleted.

'Hmm,' she murmured.

'What?' Burke asked.

'I was wondering who Steve and Eleonora's father was, and decided to check, but the register doesn't have his name.'

'Maybe he's unknown,' Burke suggested.

'If that was the case, they would have written: "Father unknown." What is on their birth certificates is just a blank space.'

'Let me see,' Burke said, staring at her laptop screen. He was also surprised. 'Well, that's interesting. Why did someone will delete the father's name?'

'Shortly before I married Steve, RAN called me and told me that there were blank fields in his file.'

'RAN checked Steve?' Sam was amazed.

'Yes. According to him, my decision to marry him was rash. Now I understand that he was right. He told me last night that there is no information yet regarding the white fields in my husband's history.'

'Let's then dig in this direction,' suggested Burke.

'I know who Steve and Eleonora's father is,' said Sam.

Cassy and Burke looked at him in surprise.

'Who is he?' Cassy asked.

'I am their father.'

'You?'

'Yes, I am Marta's ex-husband.'

'You are kidding me, right?' she said.

'No, Cassy, I'm not kidding you.'

'But how ...'

'Long story,' Sam said and started to get up.

However, Cassy and Burke blocked his way and made him sit down.

'You owe us an explanation,' she said.

'I know. It may seem strange to you, but I know as much as you do.'

'Ah, no, I don't believe you. You didn't take this lodge six years ago by accident.'

'That's right, I wanted to be closer to my daughter and my grandchildren. I even invited them here a few times. Of course, they don't know who I am. That's how I met you, Cassy, don't you remember? After that, you started coming here with Charlie, and to my delight, Steve also came from time to time.'

'That's why you asked me if I knew where Steve was when we came last night. It struck me as strange that you asked nothing else but where he is. I understand now. But why don't you tell them who you are?'

'Because I can't tell them, not yet.'

'I guess your name isn't Sam.'

'On the contrary, that's my real name. That's why I told you who I am; if you dig a little more, you would find out who the father is.'

'I'm totally confused,' said Burke, holding his head in his hands.

'Me too,' Cassy whispered.

'I promise to tell you everything, but not now. What you need to know is that I really have no idea what Steve and Eleonora have gotten themselves into, but they are definitely in a mess. I feel it, but I can't prove it.'

'And it's nothing to do with you?' Burke asked.

'No, it has nothing to do with me. Two months ago, Steve came here alone. He had told Cassy he was at his mother's. When he arrived, he looked very bad. His jeans were torn, and there were wounds on his face. He told me he had been attacked by a dog, but I didn't believe him. His wounds had nothing to do with dog bites. I tried to get him to tell me what he had gotten himself into, but he never did. All I can tell you is that while he was raving, he mentioned the name Mia several times. I tried to find out who she was, but I couldn't find anything about her.'

'Why didn't you tell me?' Cassy asked angrily.

'I wanted to tell you, but I kept thinking that maybe it was some kind of love affair, and that the woman's husband had attacked him.'

Cassy sat wearily on the sofa in front of the fireplace and she, like Burke, held her head in her hands and tried to think.

'So, you're Marta's husband,' she murmured.

'Ex-husband, yes.'

'And your name is Sam Silver.'

'Samuel Bernard Silver, but everyone calls me Sam.'

'And you're a retired cop?' Burke asked.

'Not really.'

'Weren't you a cop or retired?'

'It's complicated.'

'Yes, it's complicated,' said Cassy and went to the laptop. 'I thought my family was crazy, but your family, Sam, wins all the championships.'

Cassy and Burke were trying to find some connection, some logic to what was happening in Balkan. The two of them were drowning in a sea of information about the town and the people living in it, as well as about Steve and Eleonora. By noon, however, nothing new had appeared to give them hope that they knew something about the case.

'Whatever is going on there is not digitally documented,' Cassy finally said. 'We have to go back to Balkan and talk to the people face to face.'

'And how do you think that will happen?' asked Burke. 'If we go there, Eleonora's people will tear us apart.'

'I don't think that the two men who are chasing us are Eleonora's people. I'm starting to think that what happened yesterday was part of two different things. The mayor removed me and took another as my deputy. If she wanted to arrest me, she could have done it back then. However, the agents certainly don't mean us well. If they work for the government, they won't be able to arrest us because they won't have those rights. We already work for the Intelligence Agency and have immunity. I will call RAN to see if he can arrange something for us. We have to go back. There is no other way to find out who is against us.'

Cassy headed for the porch but then changed her mind and walked into the kitchen, where she found Sam sitting with his head down.

'Are you okay?' she asked him.

'No, I'm not well,' he admitted.

'Everything will be fine.' Cassy patted him gently on the shoulder. Then she left the room and went to call RAN. After her talk with him, she sat down on the porch bench and looked at the beautiful view before her. Sam's lodge was located on one of the peaks of the mountain and the view from that high was amazing. She could see the pine forests and the small streams that, after yesterday's rain, came down and flowed into the river. Dark rain clouds were still visible in the distance, but overall, the sky was blue, and the sun was once again warming the earth. A couple of rabbits had come to the meadow in front of the lodge. They were probably frequent visitors, because Sam's dog Buggy didn't chase them but just calmly watched them. Cassy looked at the beautiful scenery and wished she could turn back time and make it so none of it had happened. It was as if someone had pulled the solid foundation out from under her feet; it felt as if she were in quicksand. She felt much more unstable now than when Ron had died. She didn't know who she was anymore, and who her family was. She had briefly thought that Steve's family was her family too, but she had been wrong. She had also thought of Sam as a close friend, someone who understood her, but it turned out this friendship was false as well. What else would she discover, she wondered. Burke's approach interrupted her thoughts.

'What did RAN say?'

'He said he would find a house in Balkan for us to stay in. And he will send two more agents to assist us. He also asked us to include Sam in the investigation.'

'So, RAN believes him.'

'Yes. But I don't know if I believe him. I have been coming here almost every month for the past two years. I naively thought he was my friend, but now I understand that he just wanted to be closer to his son, and I was his bridge to him.'

'I'm sorry,' said Burke and, like her, he looked at the beautiful view.

'One thing I know for sure, Burke, Steve wouldn't just walk away. And where the hell is my dog?'

Cassy cried. She was angry that she was showing weakness at this moment, but she couldn't stop her tears.

'It's better to cry,' Burke told her and hugged her shoulders in a friendly way. She leaned against his chest and continued to sob. After a few minutes, her crying stopped. She got up and walked confidently to the front door of the lodge. She would find out who had torn her life apart and why, and who wanted her dead. And she would do it as quickly as possible, she promised herself.

Burke looked after her. In just a few minutes, this woman transformed before him from desperate and suffering to determined and professional. If he hadn't met Berta by now, he would surely have fallen for her, he thought, and headed inside the lodge to help her pack.

Cassy, Burke, and Sam prepared everything they needed and settled in front of the fireplace to wait for RAN to call. All three drank coffee in silence and watched the flames in the fireplace, each lost in their own thoughts. Cassy was thinking of Eleonora. She couldn't imagine her sister-in-law being involved in something and her not knowing about it. The two were very close. Cassy remembered the day she and Steve arrived in the town. They were very enthusiastic about the new beginning, which they had naively hoped would save their marriage at the time. She remembered Sully and Eleonora taking them around town and introducing them to almost everyone they met. Steve had accepted a job with an architectural firm, and Cassy had accepted the position of police chief and started working almost immediately. Sully and Eleonora had looked very happy then, and they took good care of the twins.

'There's no way they're ...' Cassy startled, realizing that she was speaking out loud.

'What's wrong?' Burke asked her.

'There is no way Sully and Eleonora are involved in anything criminal. It's like you and Berta being involved in some shady business. I would have sensed something was up.'

'Why is he hiding then?'

'I don't know, Burke, but it doesn't tie in. Eleonora is ambitious but not a bad person.'

'But she tried to poison you,' Burke reminded her.

'Maybe she didn't know what was in the water bottle,' suggested Sam.

'She is your daughter; of course, you will protect her,' replied the fireman.

'No, Sam is right. Now that I think about it, why would she give me poison when she's driving, and with her kids in the car? If I had drunk more, I would have died before their eyes. Eleonora would not allow that. There is no way she would do that.'

'Did you ask her where she got the water bottle?'

'I thought about doing it, but she fired me.'

'Talk to her when we arrive in Balkan,' suggested Sam.

'I will,' Cassy said. She looked at the fireplace, but the fire was already out. It was late afternoon, and the temperatures had risen. She decided to go out on the porch. Burke followed her.

'I'll call Berta. I hope she has calmed down and won't tease me too much,' he said and went down to the big meadow in front of the lodge. Cassy watched him talk on the phone with his wife and smiled. Berta was calm, she thought. She wished she had someone to call, too. Actually, she could have called her parents, but she knew that the moment she mentioned that she was working for the Intelligence Agency again, they would kick her ass. Instead, she put her feet up on the comfortable bench and gazed out at the beautiful scenery.

RAN's call startled her.

'You can go down to the city. I sent you the address of the house you can use.'

'Any news from Zlotov?' she asked.

'Yes, he was with his girlfriend. He will also work with you.'

'So, we will be four agents, plus Sam and Zlotov. Aren't we a big team for this small town?'

'The town is small, but my intuition tells me that something big is happening in Balkan.'

'Any ideas?' she asked.

'At least two. Human trafficking or big money laundering. There are twelve banks in the city. Have you ever wondered why there are so many?'

'No,' she admitted. 'You may be right; I'll check their employees. And why do you think there might be human trafficking? The town is not close to any borders and is almost nowhere in the middle of the mountains.'

'The mountain, Cassy, is a haven for traffickers of all origins. Large, unsupervised territory with little chance of meeting anyone. They may use the town as a base to travel to Rila. The distance is not great.'

'But where would the traffickers hide people?' she said, and even before RAN answered her, she knew the answer. 'The empty buildings. That's why someone needed the plans from the Archive Warehouse.'

'That's what I thought too, but I have no proof.'

'Now I understand why you want more people to participate in the investigation.'

'Marina can also help you with information but be careful with her. She has a habit of talking when she shouldn't,' said RAN with a laugh.

'You know her well.'

'Yes, we have known each other for a long time. Now get ready and be careful. We still don't know exactly what we're dealing with.'

'I'll be careful,' Cassy promised and almost regretted that she had to leave the lodge.

Two hours later, the three were traveling to Balkan. Sam and Burke would stop by and drop off their stuff at Burke's house, and Cassy would stay with Marina again. The old woman hugged her when she saw her at the door.

'I was very worried about you,' she said.

'I know. Now you don't need to worry. I'll take a quick shower and head out. You lock the front door after me and don't open it to anyone you don't know.'

'Okay,' Marina agreed. She was just about to say something, but Cassy didn't give her a chance to speak but quickly entered the bathroom. She couldn't wait to wash all the dirt off herself. Not only from her body, but also from her thoughts. She was so confused. She turned on the hot shower, and instead of washing herself, she just sat on the tiles and let the warm drops wash over her.

'I can't have missed all this,' she said to herself. 'Human trafficking, illegal banking operations? What was I thinking? *You're a fool, Cassy, a fool.*'

She bent her knees and rested her head on them. The warm shower continued to wash over her, and little by little, she began to relax. Maybe she had missed something, she thought, but now she was being given a chance to make things right, and she was going to do it. What puzzled her the most was why her sister-in-law and Sully, if they knew something was wrong in town, didn't ask her for help? And this lawyer, Leslie, what was she involved in? Besides the affair with Steve, there was something else going on with her. Why else would Sully risk going into her house?

Cassy calmed down, stood up, washed her hair and body quickly, and with a few ideas already in her head, she left the bathroom.

'You look better,' Marina told her.

'And I feel better.' Cassy smiled at her.

Half an hour later, Sam, Burke, Cassy, and Zlotov were sitting in the living room of the house they had been given as an office, discussing how to begin the investigation.

'I'll go with Sam to look at the empty buildings whose files were stolen,' offered Burke.

'Be careful, if RAN is right and it is a matter of human trafficking, they may not want to leave witnesses.'

'We'll be careful,' Burke said, motioning for Sam to join him.

'I'll call Eleonora and ask her to come here,' Cassy said.

'And I'm going to check the files on everyone who works in the twelve banks,' said Zlotov, and opened his laptop.

'Okay. So, we have a plan. Burke, call me before you enter any building. Don't do anything risky.'

'We will only look around tonight; we won't go inside.'

'Great.'

The two men walked out, and Cassy reached for her phone. She had to make her sister-in-law come of her own accord. She hoped the nanny would still be with the twins and Eleonora would come alone. To Cassy's surprise, she picked up the phone almost immediately.

'Eleonora, it's me,' Cassy whispered.

'Cassy? Where are you? I was worried about you.'

'I'm in Balkan, and I want to talk to you.'

'Where in town are you?'

'I'll send you the address. Can you come alone?' Cassy asked, feeling her hands shake with tension.

'Yes, I'll be with you in ten minutes.'

'Great. See you soon then.'

'See you soon.'

Cassy looked at the phone. It had been too easy.

'Zlotov, I don't want Eleonora to know that there is someone else in the house. It is best if you move to the other room and try not to make any sound.'

'Okay, boss. What if she attacks you?'

'Then you will come, of course. But if there is no danger, do not appear. Do you understand?'

'Yes,' promised Zlotov. Then he took his laptop and moved into the next room, leaving the door slightly open.

Shortly after, there was a knock on the front door. Cassy peered through the small window and recognized Eleonora's silhouette.

'Come in.'

'I thought you were staying with Marina?'

'That's right. Sit down, I want to ask you a few questions.'

Eleonora sat up and looked at Cassy. 'You don't look good,' she said. 'You need a break.'

'I will rest when I can. Now, I want to ask you something, and I want you to answer me frankly.'

'If it's about Steve cheating on you, I knew about it, but I didn't want to tell you. I begged him to stop seeing this woman, but he ...'

'It's not about cheating,' Cassy interrupted her. 'It's about the town. What's going on in Balkan, Eleonora?'

Her sister-in-law was troubled by this question. One of her hands gripped the fingers of the other tightly, and Eleonora's lips began to twitch slightly.

'Why do you think something is happening in the town? Because I fired you?'

'No, but we will get to that. Where is Sully?'

Eleonora's face paled. She started to get up from the chair, but Cassy gently nudged her back into her seat.

'He was seen looking for something in Leslie's house during the fire. I'm sure he hasn't left you, and you knew where he was all along. Now, don't lie to me. Tell me where he is. I want to speak to him.'

Eleonora looked at her with fear in her eyes. Cassy expected her to say something, but the mayor was silent.

'If you are in danger, tell me. You know you can count on me. I'm sure that's why you asked me to work for you.'

Eleonora remained silent, but Cassy felt she was on the right track. She sat down close to her sister-in-law and put a friendly arm around her shoulder.

'Do you remember the water bottle you gave me when I was discharged from the hospital?'

'The doctor recommended you drink more fluids.'

'Where did you get it?' Cassy asked.

'It was in ...' Eleonora stammered. 'It was in my handbag, but now that I think about it, I don't remember that I left it there.'

‘There was liquid nicotine in that bottle. The morning after I drank from it, I almost died,’ Cassy told her.

‘What? Was the water poisonous?’

Eleonora was horrified, and Cassy could see it in her eyes. She hadn’t put the poison in, and now Cassy’s investigation was headed in a different direction. She was most likely not the target, but her sister-in-law.

‘I could have given the bottle to one of my children!’ cried Eleonora.

‘That’s right. Someone wanted to attack us, and I’m convinced that you’re part of it. So, tell me what’s going on. I can help you. I don’t work for you anymore; I work for the Intelligence Agency. I can protect you, but you have to tell me what’s happening in the town, Eleonora.’

‘I have to go,’ said her sister-in-law. She pushed Cassy away and hurried out the door.

What the hell is going on? Cassy wondered.

‘She is very scared,’ said Zlotov, entering the room.

‘She’s terrified.’

‘Will she come back?’

‘I don’t think so. Whatever she knows, she won’t tell me. We will have to find out the truth for ourselves. One thing I did find out, though – Sully is here in Balkan. If we find him, maybe he will give us answers to some questions.’

Cassy’s phone rang, interrupting their conversation.

'Burke, any news?'

'Two of the buildings have certainly not been entered by anyone for years. We are currently in front of the third building we are checking, and there is light inside.'

'Tell me the address. Zlotov and I will come to you and take a look.'

Burke directed her to where he and Sam were. After a few minutes, Cassy and Zlotov joined them. The building was an abandoned leather goods warehouse, at least according to the documents. The front door was iron and had a large padlock attached to it.

'If someone has been inside, they didn't use the main entrance,' whispered Zlotov.

'You pass on the left and look around,' suggested Cassy. 'We will pass on the right.'

The four started at the same time, walked slowly around the building, and met at the same place.

'We didn't see anything suspicious,' Burke said.

'And we didn't see anything out of the ordinary. But why is the building lit inside? Has a light been left on?' wondered Sam.

'I have an idea,' said Zlotov. 'We can check the electricity bill. If it has been the same for several months, then most likely, the owners forgot to turn off the lights. However, if there is a difference, it means that the warehouse has been used.'

'Great idea, Zlotov. We will check the gas and electricity bills not only of this building, but also of all the abandoned ones in the vicinity,' said Cassy.

The four of them retreated slowly and returned to the house, where Zlotov immediately checked the information they needed.

'In two of the buildings, the consumed electricity is more than it should be,' he said. 'But that doesn't mean anything. The owners may only use them occasionally.'

'We have to check,' Sam said.

'It won't be tonight. We'll wait for the other two agents as well. Zlotov, please send us the files of the owners of the buildings.'

'Right away, boss.'

Burke and Cassy read the first file. However, there was not much information in it.

'The building we were in is owned by Rob Curtis. He bought it from Neil Kristoff six years ago. Zlotov, trace the gas and electricity bills from four years ago. Also, Curtis's finances.'

'Okay, boss.'

'The other building is Steve Silver's ...' Burke began to read and, realizing that this was the name of Cassy's husband, immediately stopped reading.

'Whose?' she asked in disbelief. Sam approached Burke and was trying to look at the information on his laptop.

'Steve's,' Burke confirmed and continued reading. 'He bought it four years ago from Neil Kristoff.'

'Zlotov.'

'Shall I check on Steve, boss?'

'Yes, check my husband's finances. Also, find all information about Neil Kristoff.'

'Okay, boss.'

'I'm checking Neil's file,' Burke called. 'He sold all three of his properties four years ago and moved.'

'Where does he live now?'

'No information about his current address is listed here.'

'We used to track addresses through driving licenses,' Sam called.

'Yes, we do this now too. His last address is his house in Balkan, but he sold it. So, I'm afraid we have another missing person.'

'Four years ago? How come no one has looked for him yet?' Cassy was surprised.

'He may not have changed his address on the driving licence. Many people do it for different reasons.'

'Both his driving license and his passport expired two years ago. He did not renew them,' said Burke. 'He just disappeared.'

Sam walked over to Cassy and tapped her lightly on the shoulder.

'What has Steve gotten himself into?'

'I don't know, Sam, but I'm sure Sully and Eleonora do. Burke, can you verify the ownership of the six abandoned buildings that were set on fire? I know the name Rob Curtis from somewhere.'

'I'll look into it now.'

'There's no way these buildings belong to Rob,' answered Zlotov, staring at the monitor in front of him. 'I knew Rob; we were friends. Rob fell off a cliff eight years ago. He broke his spine and died on the spot.'

'Someone took advantage of his name then,' said Sam.

'I don't know why, but I have a feeling that the lawyer is somehow involved in this whole story,' Cassy said and sighed heavily. She felt like she had never felt before – dirty. She wanted to go somewhere far away and never come back.

'Steve owns two more empty buildings,' Burke called.

'An architect and a lawyer,' Sam whispered.

'What do you mean?' Cassy asked him.

'A few years ago, two people came to the lodge who were talking about the "architect and lawyer" scheme. I hadn't heard of such a financial scheme and didn't think much of it at the time, but for some reason, I just remembered it. Steve is an architect, and Leslie is a lawyer. Maybe their relationship wasn't just romantic.'

'You think they are some kind of business partners?'

'Yes. Steve was never ambitious, but he always wanted to be rich. At least that's what he told me while we were drinking one night at the lodge. That's what he talked about all the time, actually. He wasn't talking about other women, about affairs and relationships, but about deals. Then I wondered what deals an architect could have in a small town like Balkan. I told myself that when a person drinks, sometimes he starts to dream and fantasize. But now I wonder if that's what Steve had in mind.'

'We need to talk to Leslie early tomorrow morning. Also, once the other two agents arrive, we will go to the empty warehouses that Steve bought. I am his wife, and I have the right to enter there without a warrant,' said Cassy. Steve never stopped surprising her. She was more likely to forgive him for infidelity than for an illegal business behind her back. She began to dig into his financial documents and hit the keys so hard that she caught the attention of the three men in the room.

'Calm down,' Burke told her. 'We'll find out what's going on.'

Sam was sitting next to her, looking over her shoulder at the bank statements. At first reading, there was nothing to worry about, but then Cassy caught a recurring payment order for £1000 every six to seven days. She coloured the payments red and looked for the source.

'Red Snow Ltd,' she said. 'This is the company that has been regularly transferring money into Steve's bank account. Let me know if you come across this company somewhere in the other documents.'

'I have it,' called Zlotov. 'Transactions have been made to Neil Kristoff.'

'How long ago?' Cassy asked.

'Most recently, last month.'

Sam was surprised. 'But he has disappeared and has no documents?'

'Neil Kristoff has a functioning bank account in one of the banks in the town,' said Zlotov.

'Which bank?' Cassy asked.

'KKS Bank.'

'Check if Steve has an account there too.'

'He has an account and regular payments every week of £9,999.'

'Bastard,' Cassy hissed through gritted teeth. 'How much is the account balance?'

'Zero. Steve withdrew the money immediately after the fire.'

'And there is no money in this account. He took everything and disappeared. He took Charlie with him.' Cassy's voice trembled. She was furious with her husband.

'I know it's not nice to talk about my son like that, but I think he took Charlie as a bargaining chip. At some point, he will use the dog for his own purposes.'

'Steve loves Charlie and wouldn't use him.'

'He used you, his sister, and his brother-in-law; why not the dog?' called Zlotov.

There was silence in the room. Cassy stared at the bank statement in front of her and wondered how she hadn't seen all this a few days ago. A few thousand pounds a month was a hefty sum. If she had focused and looked more closely at the paperwork, she would have known something was wrong.

'Don't blame yourself,' called Burke. 'You barely survived the fire, and being almost killed doesn't help with concentration.'

'I wonder if he tried to suffocate me with the pillow in the hospital.'

'You would have known if it was him. After all, he is your husband; you know how he smells, how he moves, how he breathes. You know him well, Cassy.'

'That's right, you're right. Someone else was there. Someone who smelled like machine oil. Steve doesn't like to get his hands dirty.'

'Boss, Red Snow Ltd was registered four years ago, and the address for correspondence in one of their contracts is Leslie's address.'

'So, we're on the right track,' Cassy said. 'We'll go talk to her tomorrow morning. It's getting late, and she's certainly not in her office. We have nothing official to warrant visiting her at home, so we will have to wait until tomorrow. Now we'd better all go home and rest. One of us must stay here and guard the documents. Nothing should leave this office.'

'I will stay,' offered Zlotov.

'Great. Tomorrow morning at seven o'clock, we will meet Leslie. I'll bring coffee,' Cassy said and headed for the door.

'Sam and I will walk with you,' Burke suggested, and the three of them left the house together. They walked two blocks without speaking. Then Cassy's phone rang and broke the silence.

'I'm on the street right now,' she told RAN. 'I'll be home in a little while and tell you what we found.'

'Who stayed in the office?' he asked.

'Zlotov is there.'

'I sent you a package; only you can read the information inside.'

'Okay, I'll do it tomorrow morning.'

'No, Cassy, you have to go back and get the package,' insisted RAN.

'Okay. I'll go back then.'

Cassy returned to the office and waited with Zlotov for the agents to arrive.

'Obviously, I won't be coming home tonight,' she told him. 'Go home if you want to. I'll see you tomorrow morning.'

'I won't leave you alone, boss. I'll stay with you. Maggie is on the night shift anyway.'

'She is a very good girl.'

'Yes, she is.' Zlotov smiled.

'Have you proposed to her yet?' Cassy asked.

'I did. Last night.' He laughed happily.

'I understand from your smile that Maggie accepted.'

'Yes. I can't believe how lucky I am.' He continued to smile.

'Congratulations,' Cassy said sincerely, truly happy for them. Everyone should experience such happiness at least once in their life. She remembered Ron's proposal. They had gone on a short vacation in the mountains. They had rented a house by a beautiful lake and were enjoying the silence and each other's company. The second morning, when Cassy woke up, Ron was out of the house, and half an hour later, he showed up with a basket of deli snacks, bagels, and croissants. He handed her a croissant and kissed her. Then he made her breakfast, and while he watched her eat, he asked her to marry him. He was an impulsive man, and she liked that very much. There was no getting down on one knee or a diamond ring, just breakfast and a question. For Cassy, it was the most romantic proposal she had ever heard of, and of course, she had said yes. She loved Ron so much that she would have lived with him on Mars. The memory made her smile. She missed Ron. She still found it hard to live without him. Steve had filled part of the void in her life during the years they had been together, but there would always be a part of her that would remain unfilled. A place that belonged only to him, to Ron.

A soft knock on the front door interrupted her thoughts. Cassy looked through the small window and recognized the two agents. She had worked with both of them years ago. Their names were Peter and Stanislav.

'We understood that you got involved in some kind of mess,' said Peter instead of a greeting.

'That's right,' she said and smiled nervously.

'So, we have come to the right place then.'

'Yes. Welcome.' She invited them inside and introduced Zlotov.

'RAN said to deliver this package to you personally,' Stanislav said and kissed her lightly on the cheek.

Cassy took the package and left for home. She needed another shower and sleep. She wasn't worried about waking Marina. Cassy was pretty sure that just putting the key in the door would wake the old woman up. And that's exactly what happened. She wasn't halfway down the corridor when the door opened, and Marina appeared wearing an old nightgown.

'Are you hungry?' she asked.

'Now that you ask me, yes. I had no time to eat dinner. I'll have something to eat after I shower.'

'I will make you a sandwich,' said the old woman and entered the kitchen.

Cassy took clean clothes from the ones Eleonora had given her and headed to the bathroom. Then she remembered the package and decided to take it with her. RAN's insistence had awakened her vigilance. The phone and important information were not to leave her sight, he had taught her.

After taking a shower, she went into her room and opened the package. Its contents spilled loudly onto the ground, making Cassy jump. She had expected documents, not flash drives and old DVDs. She crouched down and took a closer look at everything spilled on the floor. There was no name on the flash drives, but the two DVDs had Neil Kristoff's name written on them. This was the guy who had sold Steve the warehouses. Cassy could easily look at the information on the flash drives, but for the DVDs, she had to find a DVD player. Assuming Marina wasn't asleep yet, she went and knocked on her door.

'I'm in the kitchen.'

Cassy walked into the kitchen to find Marina working on a crossword puzzle.

'I thought you went to bed,' she said and sat down in the chair next to her.

'I can't sleep. After the fire, I only have nightmares.'

Marina got up and turned on the kettle. The noise of boiling water stopped Cassy from saying anything. After the water boiled, Marina took two cups and put a tea bag in each one. Then she handed one of the cups and a plate with a cheese sandwich to Cassy and gestured for her to drink and eat.

'The tea is a decoction of herbs to relax the nerves. I think after the past few days, we both need it.'

'You're right. I definitely need something to help me relax and focus.'

'You look exhausted, Cassy,' said Marina, sitting down on one of the chairs.

'I've been told that a lot lately.'

'Why don't you take a few days off? It will do you good.'

'Right now, is not the time for a vacation. I need to find who set the town on fire.'

'You're right, somebody has to find out what is happening in Balkan. People are very scared, Cassy. They hid like mice in their holes and are afraid even of their own shadows.'

'I know. I noticed the panic in their eyes today when they saw us coming back to town with Burke.'

The two women stood like that for a while, each lost in thought. Cassy then asked Marina to call her nephew in the morning and ask him to help them with a DVD player.

'I'll write you down the address to take it to,' Cassy said before going back to her room. She wondered whether to look at the information on the flash drives now or leave it for the morning, but then she finally opened the laptop and began to look at the documents attached to one of the flash drives. Most were bank statements that Cassy had already seen, but a few of the files caught her eye. They were sales contracts for several properties. What surprised her most was the price they were bought for. Only £5 per property. Who would sell their property at such a price, and how was it even legal? Steve and Leslie were really playing a big game. Both of their names were on the documents, and that didn't surprise her. However, it was more likely that the two had bought the properties for someone else. Cassy had worked on these kinds of deals while working for RAN. There was always someone behind such illegal activities. Who was driving things, and why had Steve stepped down? He was hardly that stupid to think that he would be able to get rid of his invisible "partner" so easily. *As well as me.*

Cassy gritted her teeth furiously as she thought of her husband. He was already her ex-husband, though Steve didn't know it yet. The first thing she would do the next morning was file for divorce. She didn't want to be tied to his criminal activities. The mark he had put on her would be like a brand. She would never forgive him, *never*. The two had nothing to share anyway. *Only*

Charlie, she thought and realized that Sam was right – Steve would try to use the dog as a bargaining chip. But what would he want in return? Whatever it was, she would give it to him. She couldn't lose her dog. She wouldn't be able to survive that.

Cassy took a sip of the tea she'd brought with her and changed flash drives. Before opening the files on the second one, she sighed and wondered what other surprises awaited her. When she opened the first file, she gasped – Leslie, Steve, Sully, and Eleonora had been photographed at her sister-in-law's house, and the photo was dated two days before the fire.

'*What the hell is going on?*' she muttered to herself and continued to look at the rest of the photos, the contents of which were similar. The four were obviously talking about something. Cassy saw in one of the pictures Sully getting up, and his face was angry. In the next picture, he was gone, and only Steve, his sister, and the lawyer were left in the room. Cassy wondered why the photographer had taken pictures instead of video. That was the first thing she would ask RAN in the morning. If there was a video, they could show it to someone who could lip read and figure out what the four of them were talking about. However, from the still pictures, Cassy could only assume that the meeting had not gone as planned and Sully had left the house angry. Cassy decided she needed to find him as quickly as possible. Whatever was going on, he was involved. The other person she felt she could quickly break under more thorough questioning was Leslie. This woman certainly knew more than she had told them last time.

Finally, Cassy's thoughts turned to Eleonora. Although she could see her husband's angry expression, her sister-in-law's face showed no such emotion.

She seemed calm. Maybe she didn't expect what would happen in just a few days, or maybe she was one of the initiators of the fires in the town. Whatever it was, Cassy had been very successfully kept out of the way. How had she not noticed what was going on around her? Had she lost her instinct after her last partner, Billy's death? No, she hadn't lost her instinct, she thought. In fact, if she had looked in that direction, she would have known immediately that something was wrong, but she had simply gone with the flow and let the small town entangle her in a romantic web. The purpose of her coming to Balkan was to find her inner peace and tranquillity; that was what she had been looking for and that was why she had not paid attention to what was happening around her.

And Steve, who would have thought he could do that? Certainly not Cassy. Steve wasn't stupid, not at all, but for some reason, every time he started a business or a bigger project, things didn't work out for him. Sam was right; for years, her husband had dreamed of becoming rich and buying a house by the sea where he could enjoy his old days. Such were his plans, but not hers. Hers included a family, a home, children – maybe two or three. At first, he too was taken with this idea, but then something seemed to change, and he was no longer so enthusiastic. Cassy realized that this was one of the reasons their marriage had started to go downhill. Now Steve had the money of his dreams, or so the amount withdrawn from his bank accounts indicated. *Where has he retreated to?* Cassy wondered. He probably already had a place earmarked to rest, perhaps somewhere by the sea. She tried to remember if he had mentioned any specific place to her, but Steve had always told her he would go to the "dream place". Where was this place? Cassy had to look at his bank statements again, she decided, pushing the laptop away from her. But before that, she needed to rest. She put everything back into the folder and placed it under her mattress. She would sleep on the information. She had learned insights in this way before.

-Chapter Ten-

Smouldering Embers

Nightmares haunted Cassy all night, and finally, at 5 a.m., she decided not to try to sleep anymore. Instead, she got up and went through all the information on both flash drives again. After scrutinizing every document and every photo, she felt as if she had been caught in a whirlwind. Everything felt very confused in her mind; she had never felt like this before. She looked at the pictures on the monitor. Something didn't add up, and it bothered her. It was hard for her to connect the facts, as if many pieces of a big puzzle were missing. Or she had put them in the wrong place. Perhaps the DVDs would help her understand what was happening in Balkan.

Calmed by that thought, Cassy got up and went to the kitchen to make some coffee. Marina was already there talking to someone on the phone. When she saw her, she gestured to Cassy the pot of coffee, then put the phone away and smiled.

'Good morning,' she said. 'I was talking to Michael. He will bring the DVD player here in a few minutes.'

'Thanks for the help. Also, for the coffee.'

'The way you look, I would say that you'll need at least one more cup of coffee. Did you work all night?' Marina asked.

'No, but I had nightmares and couldn't sleep well.'

'After everything you've been through, I'm not surprised you're having nightmares. Still, it wouldn't hurt to get some rest.'

'I will do it as soon as possible,' Cassy promised, then returned to her room. Marina was a good woman but very curious. Soon she would start asking her more questions, and Cassy wasn't sure she was ready to give her the right answers. She finished her coffee, dressed, and prepared to go out.

Michael arrived just in time with the DVD player.

'I can drive you to your new office. I'll pass by on my way to the store anyway. We'll just stop by to buy some coffee from Billy's,' Michael suggested, and she willingly accepted the offer. She felt exhausted. The past few days had really taken a toll on her, both physically and mentally. A good cup of coffee from Billy's would do her good.

Cassy hadn't been through the central part of the town in the past few weeks, and the sight of the ruins there caught her off guard. The waste had already been removed, and some of the buildings were charred black. It was as if a bomb had fallen and destroyed part of the city, or as if she had fallen into a futuristic painting. Only two or three buildings were still in use, and one housed Billy's Cafe. He, as always, greeted them with a smile. *Some people don't take to changes as well as others*, she thought, and gratefully accepted the hot drink that Billy handed her.

When Cassy arrived at the office, no one was there. She called Zlotov, who turned out to be talking to an informant on the far side of the house and had watched the entrance to the office from there. Reassured that the house was being watched she retired to one of the rooms, plugged the DVD player into her laptop as Michael had shown her, and waited to see what was on the first of the discs RAN had sent her. To her surprise, a picture of an interrogation at the Intelligence Agency appeared on the screen. A man in his fifties with curly dark-brown hair and brown eyes was sitting in a chair, looking visibly nervous. The video showed the recording date and time, and Cassy was surprised to find out that the date was just over four years ago. Apparently, Neil Kristoff had not disappeared then, but perhaps afterward.

The man sat, and nothing happened for a while until another man, about thirty-five years old, came in and introduced himself as Aldan Bozni. Cassy had met Aldan twice shortly before her partner, Billy, was killed. She didn't, however, know that he worked for the Intelligence Agency. Their meetings had been about another investigation. Aldan had made a strong impression on her then, and Cassy remembered thinking that he would make a great partner for her. It wasn't that Billy was bad, quite the opposite, but she thought she and Aldan would work great together. His appearance in this video, shortly after her partner's death, shook her a little. She looked away from him and tried to focus on the two men's conversation. Neil Kristoff continued to look worried and answered Aldan's questions evasively.

'If you want protection, you will have to give me some more specific information,' said the interrogator. His voice was calm, somewhat controlled, but Cassy could tell Aldan was seething inside.

Neil seemed to play him. 'I don't know anything specific.'

'Then there is no point in this conversation.'

Aldan began gathering up the documents he had spread out on the table in front of him, and Cassy noticed Neil's hands begin to shake slightly.

'Wait,' he said. 'I'll tell you all I know. It's not much, but I hope it helps you.'

'Well, I'm listening,' Aldan said, leaning back in his chair as if waiting for Neil to start talking. However, Neil fell silent again, and this prompted the interrogator to take the documents and leave the room. The camera was left rolling, and Cassy noticed the man nervously ruffling his hair and muttering to himself. No matter how hard she tried to understand what he was saying, however, she couldn't make out a single word.

'What are you looking at?' Burke's voice startled her.

'Interview with Neil Kristoff.'

'What is he saying?' Burke asked, moving closer to take a better look at the man locked in the small room.

'Nothing for now. Bozni tried to press him but failed.'

'Who is Bozni?'

'He is our colleague.' Cassy wanted to explain everything to Burke, but at that moment, onscreen, Aldan entered the room again and sat down in the chair. Neil looked at him, and this time, he seemed to calm down.

'I'm giving you one last chance, Kristoff. If you don't tell me what you have to tell me within two minutes, I will take you away from here and return you to Balkan. My time, as well as that of my colleagues, is valuable and I have no desire to waste it in idle talk.'

'Okay. Whatever is going to happen later with me, I'd better tell you. Either way, I'm here, and they'll know I spoke to you.'

'I'm listening.' Aldan leaned forward as he spoke, like a leopard ready to pounce on its prey at any moment.

'A few months ago, a woman contacted me by phone and offered me a price for all of the properties I own in Balkan. I turned the offer down because I already had another offer from a close friend of mine, and even though her offer was better, I decided that friendship is more valuable than money.'

'When was that? How many months ago?'

'I think it was early January.'

'Okay. What is the woman's name?'

'She introduced herself to me as Lydia, but after a week she called me again, and this time she told me her name was Stacey.'

'Are you sure the same woman called you?' Aldan asked, and Cassy could see how tense he was. His shoulders were raised, and his brows furrowed.

'I am certain. A few years ago, I had eye surgery that ended up with an infection, and I lost my sight for about a year. I learned to recognize people by their voices.'

'Okay. What did she tell you on her second call?'

'She said to decline my friend's offer and accept theirs.'

'Theirs? As an offer from a company or several people?'

'I don't know, she just said "their offer". I replied that I was not interested and ended the conversation.' Neil was silent for a while.

'What happened next?' Aldan asked.

'Two days later, my friend was hit by a car and was hospitalized in critical condition. Minutes later, Stacey called me back and gave me a new offer.'

Neil fell silent again. Cassy could see the violent shaking of his hands as well as the trembling of his bottom lip.

'What was the offer?' Aldan asked, his voice seeming to startle the man across from him.

'The offer? I don't know if you will believe me or not, but the new offer was my life against the properties I own.'

Cassy took a deep breath, surprised by what she heard. Burke, who was standing next to her, frowned slightly.

'What did you answer?' Aldan continued; he seemed not surprised by what he heard.

Neil swallowed hard, then looked away and said, 'I told them it would only happen over my dead body.'

Big mistake, Cassy thought. These offers usually doom you to certain death. It was downright surprising that Neil was still alive, or at least he had been four years ago, Cassy corrected herself.

'What happened next?' Aldan asked.

'One day later, late in the evening, while I was watching a movie, a man and a woman visited me. The man limped slightly. When they entered the room, I was very scared. I thought they had come to kill me.'

'Why did you think that?'

'Because they wore masks that covered their faces.'

'What happened after they entered your place?'

'They sat calmly on the sofa, as friends sit, handed me two documents, and made me sign them.'

'Did you manage to read what was written in the documents?'

'No. The woman showed me where to sign, and the moment I did it, the man told me I had paid off my debt. I asked him what debt because I don't remember owing anyone anything, and he – I will never forget this – he laughed and said, "You owed us your life". To be honest, I peed myself with fear then. Then they left, I changed and went straight to the police. The chief of police in Balkan listened to me and brought me to you.'

Cassy stared open-mouthed, amazed at what Neil Kristoff had said. Burke had turned to her as if ready to ask her a question.

'It was not me. The previous police chief took him in and was fired almost immediately. I arrived in Balkan four months later.'

'Maybe we should talk to our colleague. What's his name?' Burke asked.

'Aldan Bozni. I know him, he is very good at his job.'

The front door opened, and Cassy and Burke hurried out of the room to see who it was.

'Good morning,' Peter and Stanislav greeted. 'Something new?'

'Nothing new,' answered Cassy, and Burke looked at her, puzzled. 'We're continuing to explore the empty buildings, if you two want to go check out the other three on Zlotov's list.'

'Okay. What will you do?' Peter asked.

'I'm working on a lead, but I'll tell you about it in the afternoon in a briefing.'

The two agents left, and Burke and Cassy were left alone again.

'RAN told me that only I should look at the package he sent me. Even you weren't supposed to know what the DVDs contained.'

'There are more?' Burke was surprised.

'Yes. There is one more.'

Cassy changed the discs and waited for a picture to appear. The room was the same, and the man was the same, but with slightly longer hair. The interrogation took place two months later. As with the previous recording, Neil Kristoff was left alone, and visibly upset. At one point, his eyes met the camera, and Cassy could see his fear in them. A minute later, Aldan entered the room and sat in the chair in front of Neil. This time, he did not introduce himself, which for Cassy meant, that the interview was informal.

'Why am I here?' Neil asked.

'We need to make some clarifications regarding your previous testimony,' Aldan told him.

'What clarifications?'

'I'll tell you in a minute. Before that, tell me how you feel in your new home? Do you like the neighbourhood?'

Something in Aldan's tone made Cassy look at her colleague's face more closely. Something was wrong. Talking about a house in an interrogation room was not normal, quite the opposite.

'I like it, but I would prefer to go back to Balkan. All my relatives and friends are there.'

'When our investigation is over, perhaps you will have the opportunity to return to the town. Before that, though, you'll be in danger there.'

Neil nodded and, seemingly relieved, leaned back and stretched his legs forward.

'What do you want to clarify?' he asked.

'I would like to clarify two things with you. The first is whether you can remember the exact dates on which the conversations took place with you. We didn't find any strange calls on the phone records.'

'I don't remember the exact days. However, I remember it was late at night because I was at home, watching a series on TV.'

'Which series did you watch, and do you remember what it was about?'

'I watched "Breath", but I don't remember the exact episode.'

'Okay, that's enough kind of a guideline.' Aldan seemed satisfied with the answer, but Cassy noticed his body leaning slightly forward again, and she assumed it was just a 'warm-up question', as they called it in management. Only now would they understand the purpose of this interrogation. She looked at the monitor and felt her heart rate rise. Something important was about to happen, and she couldn't wait to find out what. She watched as Aldan smiled nervously at Neil, asking him basic life questions. *He is like a cat stalking a mouse*, she thought. Neil wouldn't notice how he got into the trap.

'Okay, will you describe to me again what the woman looked like? Height, race, any detail at all would be helpful.'

'Tall, white, with a southern accent,' Neil said, and Cassy immediately got the impression that he said all this without even thinking. It was the quickest description of a person she had ever heard. Even she took at least a second or two to think before answering. Neil had lied in the previous interrogation, and Aldan or one of his team had found out.

'Okay. Anything else?'

'She had a silver bracelet on one hand. I remember it because she made an impression on me when she indicated with her finger where to sign the documents.'

'Okay. One more question. Where did you get a hundred and twenty thousand pounds from?' While asking the question, Aldan leaned over the table and looked Neil straight in the eyes.

The mouse went into the trap, Cassy thought, and she waited to see Neil's reaction. He was worried; his face quickly changed colour. He didn't seem to know what to say.

'Who gave you the money and when?' Aldan asked, still studying him.

'She gave the money to me. She said that's what the properties were worth.'

'Who is she?'

Neil swallowed hard, then looked Aldan straight in the eyes and shook his head. He said nothing more until the end of the interrogation. He was obviously afraid. But why all this play? Why had he sought out people from the Intelligence Agency in the first place? Cassy thought there was at least one more person who knew the answer for sure. She picked up her phone and dialled RAN.

'You have seen the records,' he said without greeting her.

'Yes. Burke looked at them too. I have a question. Why did Neil go to the police and then give false statements to you?'

'Aldan thinks they sent him to the police to find out if the former police chief in Balkan was on their side.'

'That's why they fired him without warning.'

'He was warned, but in a different way.'

'RAN, can we talk to Aldan?' she asked.

'He's working on another case, Cassy, but the moment he's free, I'll transfer him to Balkan. What you need to know is that Neil Kristoff disappeared almost immediately after this interrogation. We froze his bank accounts where the money was transferred.'

'Apparently, you haven't frozen all his bank accounts. There are two in Balkan where money is transferred monthly in his name. There have been payments made by him recently.'

'Really?'

RAN was surprised, and Cassy smiled slightly. She was rarely able to surprise her boss, and his reaction meant that she, Burke, and Zlotov had done a good job. So, her instinct wasn't gone after all.

'Send me the details, also a report on your work so far. Cassy, I have two pieces of bad news. The first is that I will need Peter and Stanislav on another case, but the moment I can, I will send someone else to help you.'

Cassy expected to hear what the second piece of bad news was, but RAN was silent.

'You said you have a second piece of bad news,' she reminded him.

'Yes. I don't know how to tell you this, Cassy, but your husband is missing for real. He's not hiding from you and his family.'

'This is not news to me, but I think Marta and Eleonora know where he is.'

'No, Cassy, they don't know. I think they can guess where he is, but at some point, his tracks disappeared.'

'I will find him. He has nowhere to hide, especially if Charlie is with him. Someone will see them ...'

'Cassy,' RAN interrupted her, 'the second piece of bad news is that Charlie is dead. We found him at the last house we thought Steve was at.'

'What?' Cassy blacked out. *He can't be dead, not Charlie.* She felt her legs give way, and Burke supported her. He helped her sit in a chair.

'Cassy?' She heard the distant voice of RAN.

'I am fine. Where did you find him?'

'In a small village, not far from Marta. I guess Steve went there after they had an argument. Charlie's body will be brought in here this morning, and you can come and collect it if you want. Take two or three days off if you need.'

'Why didn't you call me as soon as you found out?' she scolded him.

'I had to see him with my own eyes. I wanted to be sure it was your dog before I told you.'

'Yes, of course,' she said and felt her heart beat faster. 'I will ask someone to bring me to Rila, maybe Marina.'

'Haven't you got your driver's license back yet?'

'No, I didn't need a car here in Balkan.' On the day her partner had been killed, Cassy had suffered head injuries, and doctors had temporarily banned her from driving. She never contacted the doctor to get a document that would allow her to drive again.

'Okay, I'll think about how to help you in this matter.' RAN was silent again for a short time. 'And Cassy ...'

'Yes?'

'I am truly sorry for your loss.'

'They killed my dog,' she whispered and began to cry quietly. Burke reached over and took the phone from her hands, told RAN that they would call him later, and put his arms around Cassy's shoulders.

'I'm so sorry, Cassy,' he said quietly, leaving her alone with her pain.

Cassy couldn't imagine her life without Charlie. He was like her shadow, like a part of her. She felt as if someone had ripped her arm off. And it was all Steve's fault. If he were alive, she would find him and wring his neck with both hands. Then she drank the water that Burke had brought her, stood up long enough to judge whether her legs were trembling, and when she felt she stood firmly on the ground, she said to herself that she must continue to look for the culprits responsible for what was happening around her. She would take a day off to say goodbye to her dog, and then she would come back here, dig up the embers, and start such a fire that everyone involved in her dog's death would burn.

-Chapter Eleven-

A Trap

Cassy had decided to go to the capital for a day, but she actually ended up staying only a few hours. RAN had taken Charlie's body from the morgue, and they buried him in one of the Agency's cemeteries. Her dog had been shot at point-blank range. The bullet and the chip he had were removed from his body and were being analysed. Cassy hoped they would lead to a of clue. She was so overcome with her desire for revenge that if anyone looked into her eyes, they would have seen lightning in them. Her grief had turned to rage. RAN tried to talk to her about it, but she told him not to waste his words. She needed time to calm down, but she didn't have any, so she returned as quickly as possible to Balkan, and the first thing she did was hire a lawyer and file for divorce. Nothing tied her to Steve anymore, and wherever he was, if he was alive, he would know she didn't want him in her life anymore.

After she had finished with the lawyer, Cassy headed to her new office and called Marta on the way.

'Cassy, how are you?' asked her mother-in-law.

'I'm not well, Marta. They found Charlie dead. I buried him a few hours ago.'

Marta didn't say anything at first; she was clearly taking in the news.

'And Steve?' she asked.

'No one has seen him. There were no personal belongings in the house where they found Charlie.'

Marta didn't ask any more questions, which puzzled Cassy. Did her mother-in-law know what was going on? Could she be involved too? Maybe she should investigate her too. Although, according to her, Marta lived quite far away, and she hardly had anything to do with what was happening in Balkan.

As she walked to the office, Cassy also called Eleonora, but her sister-in-law didn't answer. Either she was busy, or she didn't want to talk to her anymore. Cassy would have to call her out and question her again. Eleonora was the mayor of the town; there was no way all this could have happened without her knowledge. And the photos that Cassy saw that night clearly showed that she knew about Sully's presence in town.

'I'm back.' She greeted the men in the office and immediately felt the concerned looks of Burke, Sam, and Zlotov. 'I am fine. I am upset, and I'm a little tired, but I'm fine. What did you find?'

'Hardly anything new,' said Burke, continuing to watch her carefully.

'We need to question Leslie and Eleonora,' Cassy said. 'Burke and I will go to the lawyer's office, and you two go to that warehouse again and take pictures if you can. I want to see what's inside.'

'We cannot enter without a warrant,' said Zlotov.

'You don't need it. I am the wife of the owner, and I have the right to open the warehouse.'

'You will have to come with us then. The fact that you give us permission is not enough, and you know it,' explained Sam.

'Okay. I'll come to open the warehouse, then Burke and I will go to Leslie's office after that.'

'Are you sure you don't need another day off?' Burke asked her.

'I don't need rest. I need answers,' she said and headed for the outer door. Everyone else followed her. Just before they left, Cassy remembered they were leaving the office unattended, and asked Zlotov to stay behind. She needed more people, she thought. She hoped RAN would send someone soon.

When Cassy opened the old, empty building, she was immediately hit with a musty smell. There was a dead person inside, she guessed. It could have been a mouse, she tried to reassure herself. Burke decided to look around the right side of the warehouse, and Sam and Cassy headed to the left. The warehouse was a large, empty hall, and everything seemed to be visible at a glance. At the end of the left side, however, there was a large pile of matter, and since the lighting was dim, neither Sam nor Cassy could make out what it was. However, with each step, they both could smell the rot more and more. When they reached the pile, Cassy was relieved to see a cat's corpse. Maybe someone else's pet, she guessed. Or maybe a stray cat that fell into the warehouse as if in a trap. The warehouse was well insulated and completely windowless. There was poor ventilation, only a small vent in the attic, but the cat had hardly managed to get in there.

'It's been dead for at least two days,' Burke said after examining the animal's corpse.

'So, someone was coming in then,' mumbled Cassy. 'What did they use it for?'

'Look here.' Sam pointed to something written on one of the walls. There were dates and names. He and Burke took pictures of the signs, then slowly began to look around the hall in more detail, Sam shining with his phone's light on them.

'We have to come back with better equipment,' Cassy said after they finished the inspection. It took them more than two hours to film everything. For her, there was no doubt that the premises were used for human trafficking, but there was no way to prove it. There were many "Help" signs in different languages. She shivered as she stood inside. Finally, the three got out and took a deep breath of fresh air.

'Sam, ask Zlotov to help you send all the photos to management and ask them what to do with the cat. We can come back later and check if it has a chip and find out who owns it.'

'Okay, Cassy. Call me if you think of anything else.'

'Try calling each of the phone numbers that were written on the floor and walls of the warehouse,' suggested Burke. 'That way we might find out who was inside, although they could be phone numbers from other countries.'

'We will do it,' promised Sam and headed for the office. Burke and Cassy walked in the opposite direction to Leslie's office.

The moment the lawyer saw them, she tried to lock the front door, but Burke pushed her aside and made room for Cassy to enter, then he followed her. Leslie tried to lock herself in one of the rooms in her office, but this was also unsuccessful. Finally, resigned to having nowhere to run, she headed for her desk and sat down in the chair, continuing to watch them both.

'It's illegal to trespass on someone else's property,' she said and glared at Cassy.

'It is immoral to sleep with a married man,' she replied to the lawyer.

'We just want to ask you a few questions,' Burke intervened, feeling that if he did not stand between the two women, there would be a war.

Leslie glanced briefly at him, then back at Cassy. 'Then call me in the legal way for questioning.'

'We prefer to talk to you in a more pleasant environment,' answered Burke.

'Okay. Suppose I want to talk to you, what do you want to talk about?'

'About Sully,' Cassy said, waiting to see Leslie's reaction. If she was surprised at the mention of his name, the lawyer did not show it. Her profession was such that one learned to hide one's feelings, Cassy thought, and she decided that they weren't going to be able to get any information out of her today.

'I told you he is my client, and I cannot talk about him with you.'

'Okay,' Cassy agreed and motioned for Burke to leave. Leslie looked at her in astonishment.

'What is it you wanted to ask me?'

'This and other things, but we will do it the legal way. We'll call you in for questioning as soon as possible,' Cassy told her and headed for the front door. Burke, as surprised as the lawyer, followed her.

'We could have pressed her and asked her at least a few more questions,' he said as they walked towards their office.

'She won't tell us anything. If we want to press her, we will need more evidence and facts.' Cassy hadn't mentioned to Burke the pictures she'd looked at on the flash drives. She would only tell him as a last resort. Something about these pictures bothered her, and maybe RAN was right to send them only to her. When they got back to the office, she locked herself in her new office and dialled her sister-in-law's phone again. This time, Eleonora answered.

'We need to talk in private,' Cassy said. 'I'll be waiting for you on the Mountain Path by the collapsed bridge in half an hour.'

'Okay,' Eleonora said quietly and ended the conversation.

Cassy returned to her colleagues and went over some of the photos they had taken in the warehouse. Then she told everyone she needed some fresh air and she was going for a walk, and headed for the Mountain Path. The place where she was supposed to meet her sister-in-law was only a few minutes away from their temporary office, and when she arrived, she was not surprised that Eleonora was still not there. Her sister-in-law would need more time to arrive. Cassy looked around. The Mountain Path had changed since she had last walked it. After a few days of heavy rain, the plants had turned green again, and some of the bushes had even bloomed. Clear mountain water flowed from a nearby fountain again, and Cassy felt as if she were at a turning point in life. The old, dead, and rotten had been replaced by a new, young, and fresh life. The sound of approaching footsteps interrupted her thoughts.

'Cassy,' said Eleonora quietly when she stood in front of her. 'Why this secrecy?'

'I wanted to tell you something, but it's not for the phone.'

'Okay. What is so urgent?' Eleonora had assumed a defensive posture with her arms crossed in front of her chest.

'Actually, it's two things. One is that no one knows where Steve is. Police traced him to a house in a village near Marta but did not find him there. I guess you knew about this place and thought he was safe.'

Cassy did not miss Eleonora's surprise when she heard that they had found the house where Steve had been.

'Why was he hiding there?' asked her sister-in-law, clearly deciding to continue the game of cat and mouse.

'Maybe you can tell me.'

'How would I know?'

'Of course, you know. Look, Eleonora, I'm tired of going around in circles. I'm here to find answers, and I know you can give them to me. Maybe not all of them, but you can still give me a clue as to what's going on. Why did Steve leave town? Why did he have so much money in his bank accounts? I'm sure you know what he's been up to.'

'I don't know anything,' Eleonora said.

'They executed Charlie,' said Cassy, angry at her sister-in-law's behaviour. 'Why would anyone do that if Steve wasn't involved in something?'

'What? Charlie?'

This time, Cassy felt that Eleonora's surprise was genuine.

'Yes, they killed my dog. Do you still claim you don't know what's going on in the town? You're the mayor; you should know what's happening.'

'And you were the chief of the police until recently,' Eleonora reminded her.

'That's right, but I think it all started long before I came, right?' Cassy was so angry that she punched her sister-in-law in the shoulder. 'You appointed me to this position and involved me in it without warning me. And Steve, was he in on the plan too, or did he come on board later?'

'What do you mean?' Eleonora asked with genuine confusion.

'You know very well what I'm talking about. Where's Sully? I want to talk to him.'

Eleonora rubbed her injured shoulder and looked away as if considering what to do. 'I will tell him to contact you, but I can't promise that he will do it,' she finally said. 'I really don't know what Steve has gotten himself into, but something is really going on in town. Sully knows what's going on but refuses to tell me. He is worried about our children.'

'Okay, tell him to contact me, by all means.'

'I will tell him. And Cassy ...'

'Yes?'

'I'm so sorry about your dog. I know how attached you were to him.'

Cassy nodded and headed towards the wire bridge that had already been restored. As she walked to the office, she wondered why she had decided to speak to Eleonora on her own. She could have taken Burke or Zlotov with her. Perhaps she had still hoped that her sister-in-law was telling the truth and did not know exactly what was happening in Balkan. However, everything found in the warehouse gave the clear impression that the city was being used for human trafficking. Were the people being taken to the capital or to the border? she kept asking herself. And what did Sully know? She had to find him and talk to him first, privately. It wasn't that she didn't trust Burke and

Zlotov, but Sam still bothered her. Any father would protect his children, and Cassy didn't want her and Sully to come between them.

When she returned to the office, Zlotov told her that they had found a chip in the cat. Her owner lived near the warehouse and had been looking for the pet for five days. Then, most likely, the animal unwittingly fell into this trap. If a cat couldn't get out from there, how could the people who were inside escape? They were all trapped, Cassy thought, and it dawned on her to think what those people had been through there. In one of the photos, human excrement was clearly visible in a corner. They could not even use a toilet. And did the people who were there eat at all? Did they drink water?

Cassy once again reproached herself that this was all happening right under her nose, and she had no idea about it. Was human trafficking the reason Charlie had been executed? Her eyes watered again with grief. She retreated to her office and sobbed softly. When she gathered herself, she felt that someone had approached her. She looked up and, to her surprise, saw Aldan watching her. He didn't say anything; he just leaned down and hugged her. His gesture calmed her down.

'RAN said you were working on another case,' she said quietly, embarrassed by her tears and the private moment in which he had caught her.

'This morning, we finished the other case, and RAN immediately sent me to help you. I called you to tell you I was coming, but you didn't answer the calls.'

Cassy nodded. She had put her phones away. She wanted to calm down first before she started working again.

'Come on, I think we both need some fresh air,' he offered, and Cassy remembered why she had wanted him as a partner. He seemed to read her mind, and as they investigated together, the two complemented each other very well.

'Let's first find out if others have discovered anything new. Then, while I'm showing you the city, I'll tell you what we came across.'

'RAN gave me all the information,' said Aldan.

'He didn't tell you everything. I didn't even have time to send him my new report. You can help me with that later.'

'Granted,' he agreed and followed her into the next room.

Sam, Burke, and Zlotov continued trying to find out who had been in the warehouse and called the phone numbers written on the floor and walls inside the building.

'So far, the mission has been unsuccessful, boss,' said Zlotov. 'RAN promised to send people to take samples and physical evidence.'

'Maybe we should go check out the other two warehouses that Steve owns,' Burke suggested.

'We will go as soon as Aldan and I return from a walk.'

'What do you think happened in that warehouse?' Aldan asked Cassy as soon as they left the office.

'Do you know what I think happened? I think someone set all these people in a trap. In a trap from which it was difficult for them to escape, and therefore everywhere you look in this warehouse, there is a cry for help.'

'And you think your husband has something to do with it?'

'I am sure. And soon Steve will be my ex-husband.'

'You didn't decide to kill him, did you?' Aldan asked in amazement.

'No, I will divorce him.'

Aldan sighed in relief. If it were him, he would want to kill the son of a bitch. He and Cassy walked for a while in silence, then she quickly told him about the town and its people. When they reached the burned buildings, she sat down on one of the ruins and relayed to him all the information they had gathered so far. The only thing she didn't share with him was her last conversation with Eleonora. By the time they got back to the office, it was already late. Burke suggested that he stay in the office and stand guard, and that everyone else go home. They agreed to meet early in the morning at one of the warehouses and see what surprise awaited them there.

-Chapter Twelve-

Bound Bodies

The alarm clock woke Cassy, and she struggled out of bed. She had cried most of the night for Charlie, and every time she closed her eyes, she could see his bloody fur. Then she dreamed that the two of them were engulfed in the flames. When she opened her eyes, she saw that her hands were shaking slightly. Cassy knew she was mentally unstable at the moment, but she didn't want to admit that to her colleagues. If she mentioned anything, she would be immediately removed from the investigation, and she was the only person who knew the people who were involved well. *Do I even know them?* she wondered. She pushed back the covers and got out of bed. It was only half past five, but Cassy heard Marina making coffee in the kitchen. This woman barely slept. When she joined her at the table, there was a sandwich and coffee waiting for her.

'You know I'm not your child, and you don't have to make me breakfast?' said Cassy.

'Let's pretend that you are my stepdaughter, if that will make you feel better,' said Marina and handed her a plate with sliced cheese. 'Eat, you need energy after the long hours of work.'

'Thank you,' Cassy said. She got up from her chair and hugged the old woman. Marina patted her on the back and then pointed to the food.

'Eat,' she ordered, and Cassy gratefully sipped her coffee and took a bite of her sandwich. She really needed to eat more, but during the day, she had no time.

At five minutes to six, she left the house and headed for the warehouse where she had agreed to meet Burke and Aldan. Sam had stayed the night in the office, and Zlotov was to join him a little later.

'Did you sleep well?' Aldan asked her when he saw her approaching.

'Not really,' she admitted, then walked past him and stood in front of the warehouse door. To her surprise, the door didn't have a padlock but was locked with an old type of lock that Cassy hadn't seen in years.

'How are we going to open it?' she asked, giving Burke and Aldan a chance to look around the door.

'It won't be easy,' answered Burke. 'These locks are very strong. I think we should cut part of the door.'

'It won't be necessary.' Aldan smiled. He dialled Zlotov and asked him to find him a screwdriver. When Zlotov brought the screwdriver, Aldan began to unscrew the bolts of the lock.

'How did you know how to do that?' asked Burke, and he looked at his new colleague with respect.

'My father had a garage with old classic cars, and he didn't allow us to go in there,' explained Aldan. 'However, my friend Andrew and I entered several times without him noticing. We would unscrew the lock, go into the garage, and when we were done. screw the lock back. Until he caught us.'

'What did he say to you when he caught you?' asked Zlotov.

'He slapped us a few times. The only time he ever did it. Then he replaced the old lock and put a bell on the new one to alert him when someone entered or left the garage.'

'Cunning,' laughed Zlotov.

'Yes, my old man was clever. Here, it's done,' said Aldan, taking apart the disassembled lock and slowly opening the warehouse door.

It was getting light outside, but it was dark inside the warehouse, and when the four first entered, they could see almost nothing. Even so, with the first two steps, Cassy shivered. The smell was unbearable, and there was a slight whispering sound from inside the warehouse. Aldan and Burke illuminated the wall with the flashlights they carried and looked for the light switch. When they found it and the lights came on, they all took a step back in amazement at the sight before them. Dozens of pairs of eyes were staring at them. There were people clustered at the far end of the warehouse. Cassy adjusted to the light and saw, with horror, that they were attached to a wire hanging from the ceiling.

'God,' she muttered, and she immediately dialled RAN.

'Send reinforcements and some medical teams,' she told him. Then she took two photos and sent them to him.

'Shit,' she heard him say on the other end of the phone. 'Stand there and do nothing.'

'RAN, there is one more warehouse we need to check,' said Aldan.

'Go there with Cassy. Where are Zlotov, Burke, and Sam?' asked RAN.

'Sam is in the office; Zlotov and Burke are here.'

'Okay. Cassy and Aldan, go to the other warehouse and be careful. Burke and Zlotov, stay with the people, but don't untie them yet. It is possible that if you release them, they will attack you, so you'd better wait for us. I will send two helicopters with reinforcements and medics. I will come too. Cassy, call me to let me know what's in the other warehouse.'

'I will,' she whispered, still looking at the people in front of her. There were more than twenty of them, she counted quickly, and they all looked miserable. *God, how is all this possible*? she wondered, and with difficulty, she looked away from them. They had to go as soon as possible to open the other warehouse. She went out, and Aldan followed her, taking her elbow lightly as if to support her.

'I'm fine,' she told him.

He released her and let her catch her breath. 'You are not fine, Cassy, but we must go on. I promise to give you a chance to rest a little later.'

'I am fine. I'm just surprised, that's all.'

'Well, if you say so.'

He didn't believe her, and Cassy was left with the feeling that she couldn't hide anything from him. It was as if he could read her mind.

'The other warehouse is two blocks away,' she said and started in that direction. Aldan followed her, letting her lead the way. He was giving her time to recover, she thought.

While working for the Intelligence Agency, Cassy had come across all kinds of cases. Mostly corruptions and murders. People she investigated were often found dead, and while she respected human life, she did not suffer or feel much sympathy for them. Not in this way. Now, seeing these suffering people, Cassy felt like her heart would burst. Who were they, and why were they bound like that? What human being deserved to be put in a warehouse like this and treated like this, she wondered. *Freaks*, the people who did this were freaks. Cassy took a deep breath and tried to release the emotion as she had been taught. She closed her eyes and let the light from the rising sun wash over her. Aldan stood close to her but didn't make a sound when she stopped, as if understanding what was going on inside her. Cassy was grateful for that. She stood like that for another minute or so, then she signalled to him that she was feeling better and turned down the street on which the warehouse was located.

When they arrived, they saw that the door was slightly ajar. Aldan pushed Cassy behind him and slowly opened the iron door. To their surprise, there was no one in the warehouse. It was empty, and, unlike the other two warehouses, this one smelled of cleaning supplies and bleach.

Cassy went inside and started looking around. All she found were a few letters, apparently slipped under the door by the postman, and a business card that was visible under one of the shelves. This warehouse was small and seemed to be used as an office, at least, that was how Cassy felt as she looked around at the two desks that were facing the ground. The letters were addressed to Red Snow Limited.

'Someone is trying to cover their tracks,' said Aldan, and this time he called RAN. After talking to him, the two returned to the other warehouse and waited for reinforcements to arrive. A crowd of onlookers had already gathered around the building, and a few minutes later, Eleonora arrived as well, together with the new chief of police. After failing to extract any information, they both left with a promise to return again. Cassy refused to speak to her sister-in-law. The thought that Steve was involved in all of this, and that Eleonora probably knew about it, haunted her all the time. However, according to Cassy, there was a missing piece of the puzzle. Someone was behind this whole trafficking scheme, and she couldn't guess who. A few years of idleness in the small town had dulled her intuition.

As they waited outside the warehouse, Cassy was thinking about Aldan as well. She had never gotten around to asking him what he knew about the case. Perhaps Neil had told him something outside of the interview, or perhaps her colleague had discovered something during the investigation itself. Aldan was very good at his job, and now that she could feel his presence next to her, she felt as if she was more protected. She trusted Burke, and somewhat trusted Zlotov, but Sam's kinship with Eleonora and Steve worried her. Cassy had decided to discuss his further involvement in the investigation with RAN.

'What's bothering you?' Aldan's voice startled her. He had moved closer to her and whispered his question in her ear.

'Sam,' she admitted, and he nodded.

'RAN told me he was the father of Steve and the mayor of the town.' Aldan looked like he wanted to continue talking, but at that moment, reinforcements arrived. Cassy took advantage of the buzz around her and snapped a few random photos of the crowd of onlookers. Perhaps one of them was involved and watching what would happen next. Burke noticed she was taking pictures, and a satisfied smile appeared on his face. Only the camera on his phone was sticking out of his jacket pocket. She saw it and thought that he was probably taking a video of the attendees. What had Burke done for the Intelligence Agency, Cassy wondered. There was no information on this in his file, and she hadn't had time to ask RAN, but from Burke's actions at crime scenes, she had the feeling that he was on a reconnaissance mission and that his involvement was not just that of a firefighter. Had Burke come to town undercover, she wondered.

Several men from the Intelligence Agency stood outside the warehouse door and asked Cassy and her colleagues to back off. Then they went inside and cut the wires to which the people were tied, releasing each of the prisoners. They didn't understand the language, so the agents communicated through gesture, and showed them where to go. Even though they were freed, the people were still looking on in fear, and this time, Cassy saw Aldan looking into the faces of the crowd as well.

'They are looking at someone,' he whispered to her.

'Yes, but who?'

Aldan made his way to the sidewalk where the onlookers were standing, and as he approached, several people separated from the crowd and went in different directions. It was obvious to Cassy that they wouldn't be able to follow them all. *Well, it doesn't matter,* Cassy thought. They would recognize them later from the pictures they had taken with Burke.

After freeing everyone and taking them in for questioning and examination, three forensics workers entered the warehouse, and RAN gestured for Cassy, Burke, and Aldan to follow him. Zlotov had to stay on guard outside the warehouse, a job he didn't like much, but Cassy reassured him that he wouldn't have to stay long. She and her colleagues, along with RAN and two more of his team, headed to the makeshift office. As they walked, Cassy told them what they had discovered in the past few days and RAN, and Aldan listened intently.

'I don't know if I should remove you from the investigation, Cassy,' her boss said after the brief meeting.

'I know all the people here, RAN. I'll be of use to the investigation.'

'I have no doubt that you will be of use to us, but you are not in good shape. You're tired, and if it gets hot, I'm not sure you'll be able to handle the pressure. I think you need a break. Maybe it's a good idea after we're done here to take a day or two and think things through.'

'Yes, I need a break. To be honest, I haven't been able to sleep for the past few days. I imagine it would take at least a day to interview everyone we found in the warehouse. I can rest during this time and, when I'm ready, go back to work.'

RAN was thoughtful, as if considering what she had said.

'Okay,' he finally agreed. 'But if I feel that you are not in good shape, I will remove you from the investigation. You agree?'

'I agree.' She smiled contentedly. Then she asked him what they were going to do with Sam.

'I will have to remove him from the investigation,' said RAN. 'But I will keep him nearby. He might come in handy at some point.'

'Do you believe him?' she asked.

'I believe him, but I cannot ignore his fatherly feelings.'

When the four entered the office, they found Sam sitting in front of a laptop, sipping his coffee. He looked calm on the outside, but Cassy had known him for a long time now, and the throbbing of the vein in his neck betrayed his nervousness.

RAN asked Cassy, Burke, and Aldan to leave them alone, and the three retreated to the makeshift kitchen. Before going into the kitchen, Burke grabbed his laptop, and while Cassy made tea and coffee for everyone, he downloaded the footage from his phone and hers. When he was ready, the three of them stood in front of the small monitor and stared at the pictures and videos. At first glance, they all looked like they were just there out of curiosity, until in one of the photos, Cassy noticed a man with a beard who seemed somewhat familiar to her. She had stared at him while they were sitting outside the warehouse, but now that she could see his face in greater detail, she had no doubt that it was Sully. He had disguised himself well, she thought. He wore glasses, his clothes were those of an old man, and his stomach was that of someone overweight. She would never have known it was him if he hadn't taken off his glasses in one of the photos. Cassy had a feeling he had done it on purpose. She had a feeling he had revealed himself to her. But why? When they reviewed Burke's phone video, her suspicions were confirmed. Sully looked at her and took off his glasses. She took a screenshot and sent it to Zlotov, asking if Sully was still there, but Eleonora's husband had left.

'But why did he do it?' she said.

'To understand that people aren't looking at him. See here?' Aldan said and showed Cassy the three men who had left in a hurry. Sully was far away from them, watching them leave. The finger of one of his hands rose and pointed at them.

'I think he was trying to tell you something,' confirmed Burke.

'He knows who these men are. But why doesn't he contact us and tell us what he knows?' Cassy wondered.

'He probably doesn't trust us. Or rather, he trusts you but not us. Since when did you go for a walk alone, Cassy? Was there a time when you were absolutely alone without any of us accompanying you or without Marina in the house?'

Cassy thought about it. The only time she had been alone was when she went to talk to Eleonora. Burke was right; Sully would only contact her if she was alone.

'Maybe it's time for me to take a short break,' she said. She put down the cup of freshly brewed coffee and headed for the front door. At RAN's questioning look, she gestured to Burke and Aldan; they could explain to him what was going on. Her boss nodded, and Cassy walked out into the street alone. She knew exactly where to go.

It was a weekday, and most people were at work, and the children were at school. Sully was known for his love of good coffee and had always mentioned that Billy's coffee was the best in town; for that reason, he would sometimes hang out there for hours. Cassy guessed that the coffee wasn't the only reason he visited the cafe. She walked slowly down the street and felt people's looks. Some greeted her and tried to ask her questions, and others passed her with a clear coldness towards her. The gazes she felt, however, were from people behind the windows in their houses, restaurants, and shops. What did they think of her now? She used to feel their friendly smiles and goodwill, but now her presence probably caused alarm. Everything around her was collapsing, and if she were, she would be running away from herself.

When she entered the café, there were only a handful of people inside. Cassy looked around, then sat down at a table for two and ordered a coffee and a fresh orange juice. Billy took her order, and when he returned with the drinks, he placed a napkin to her right and gave her a stern look. He then turned his back on her and started a conversation with the café patrons, thereby diverting the others' attention from her. Cassy took a sip of her coffee and then lifted the napkin as if to wipe her mouth. She looked at the writing on the reverse side and crumpled it up into a ball. She looked around and saw a man leaving the café. He had been sitting with his back to her on one of the bar stools, but when she saw him come out, she recognized him. RAN was right; she was tired, and it was preventing her from concentrating. Under other circumstances, she would have recognized Sully immediately, but now it took her a few minutes, which could have been crucial.

Cassy stayed in the coffee shop for another ten minutes, and after finishing her drinks and paying, she headed to her sister-in-law's house. Sully would be there waiting for her in half an hour. Cassy wondered if she should call RAN and tell him about the meeting but decided not to risk it. Sully might be watching her, and a phone call would scare him. She moved slowly through the burned part of a city. Her path passed the block where she, Steve, and Charlie had lived until recently. The thought of them again pierced her heart as if with two different blades. She tried not to think about them and wondered if anything had survived in the flat. It had been a month and a half since the fire, and most likely, someone had already come in and taken everything away. It hadn't occurred to her to go and check what was there. She had decided that the flat had burned down and that there was nothing there. Afterwards, she decided that since the life in the dwelling was gone, she didn't need to look for anything else there, but now, as she watched the half-collapsed building, Cassy thought that she would go and see what was left. Maybe she'd find one of Charlie's toys for a keepsake, or maybe she'd find the two keepsakes she kept in a box, given to her by Ron. She absolutely had to get back to the flat as soon as possible, she promised herself, and turned down the Mountain Path toward her sister-in-law's house.

It took her more than half an hour to get there. In many places, the path had been used as a dump, and Cassy had to dodge and jump over debris. The city was no longer the romantic place she had come to live in. Now that she thought about it, she felt like the people they had found in Steve's warehouse. She felt trapped. She had entered this town, and someone had tricked her and tied her up, promising her a good and bright future. Instead, she found herself in a vortex and in a world that seemed to take everything from her. Who had set her up, Steve or Eleonora? Someone had put a piece of cheese down for her, and she, like a hungry mouse, had gotten caught in the trap, and now it was difficult for her to get out. Did Sully feel the same way? She would soon find out.

-Chapter Thirteen-

Silence

Cassy approached the door of the house and rang the bell, but no one answered. She waited a few minutes, then walked around the house, but when she saw nothing suspicious, she backed away. There was no sign of Sully. She wondered why he would set her up with a meeting if he had no intention of coming. She went on for another five minutes and finally gave up. Like on the day of the fire, she decided to cross the bridge and walk along the main road. She had almost reached the bridge when she felt someone's presence beside her.

'In five minutes, I'll be waiting for you at the end of the path,' Sully whispered to her and quickly walked away.

Cassy continued walking, but just before the bridge, she turned left. If she walked down the small alley, she would end up at the end of the Mountain

Path. Sully was being cautious, she thought. He had re-insured himself in case she had warned her colleagues that she was going to meet him. And she would have done the same if she were in his place.

A light rain fell from the sky, and the temperatures dropped a few degrees in an instant. Cassy tried to warm herself by crossing her arms over her chest. She hoped her meeting with Sully was somewhere warm. The last thing she needed was a cold. When she reached the end of the path, Cassy looked around. There was no one around. Then, on her left, just behind some tall bushes, Sully appeared.

'Come here,' he said and led her down a narrow path. They walked like this for a few minutes and ended up in a small bungalow.

Sully handed her a chair and made her sit down. Cassy shivered, unsure if it was the cold, the rain, or the place she was in.

'Don't worry, I won't hurt you,' Sully said and sat across from her. 'Eleonora told me that you wanted to meet me, but you didn't give me a chance to contact you. Your colleagues don't leave you alone.'

He smiled, and Cassy relaxed. *It's good not to let your guard down, though,* she remembered what RAN had taught her.

'Someone tried to kill me twice; it's normal for them to behave like that,' she said. 'Why are you hiding, Sully? Why all the secrecy?'

'We will get there. First, I want to ask you, did you manage to find Steve?'

'No, but my boss found Charlie dead.'

The news visibly startled Sully. His gaze darkened, and his hands balled into fists.

'Charlie?' he asked.

She nodded, and the memory of her dog's death brought tears to her eyes again. She was tired of it all. She needed to rest, go somewhere, maybe high in the mountains, or retreat to a place like the one she and Sully were in now.

He watched her and waited for her to calm down. 'Steve got involved with some dangerous people,' he finally said.

'Who are these people, Sully? Why are you hiding here?'

'I don't know who is driving things, but shortly after you came to the town, strange things started happening.'

'Such as?'

'One of the things that made an impression on me was that late at night, articulated lorries would come and enter abandoned factories. You know, as the fire chief, I had to look at these buildings from time to time. As I passed by one of them, I noticed people who didn't live in the city standing guard outside the door of one of the warehouses. I wondered why they would do that. I had gone in there a few months before for a check and knew there was nothing inside, so I went back in the evening to look again, but this time there was a padlock on the door. Then I checked the property register and saw that the warehouse was purchased by the company named Red Snow Ltd.'

Cassy nodded. The puzzle was starting to fall into place.

'The strange thing was that I could not find out what this company was doing and what they used this warehouse for. Do you remember that one day I called you and wanted to talk to you about something?'

'Yes.' Cassy remembered that day very well. She had wondered what he wanted them to talk about, then right after he disappeared.

'Well, that's what I wanted to tell you then, but then Steve's name appeared in one of the documents.'

'And you refused to talk to me because you decided that I was also involved.'

'Exactly.'

'Did you tell Eleonora what you found?' Cassy asked.

'Not right away. I told her only after I checked all the information and asked her advice on what to do. After all, Steve was her brother.'

'What did she advise you?'

'That's the strange thing; she advised me not to get involved. Eleonora knew about it, Cassy. She knew who the company was, and she knew about Steve's relationship with Leslie.'

What Sully said shocked Cassy somewhat, but at the same time, she seemed to have expected her sister-in-law to be involved in some way.

'Did she force you to withdraw?' she asked.

'Not only her. One evening, after the children had gone to bed, Steve and Leslie arrived at the house and, together with Eleonora, persuaded me to work with them. Steve told me that if the people they were working with found out that I knew anything about their dealings, they would most likely threaten me, my wife, and my children.'

'Who are these people, Sully?' Cassy asked again.

'You see, that's the point. After all these years, I still don't know who did this and how. After I refused to participate in their deals, Eleonora made me leave the house and the next day told everyone I was missing.'

'So, you didn't run away, you didn't hide; she knew where you were all this time, but still she declared you missing.'

'That's right, and when I tried to contact you, she stopped me and threatened me that I wouldn't see my children for the rest of my life. So, we made a deal. I would stay at the house every weekend. In return, she would cover my tracks to hide me from the people who wanted me dead. After a while, I began looking for a way out again, but I did not find one. Shortly after my disappearance, two men visited Eleonora and the kids and threatened her that if she did not continue to take care of their business, not only her husband but also her children would disappear. Apparently, they had believed that I had left her, but their threat haunted us for a long time.'

'But why didn't you tell me?' Cassy asked.

'Eleonora was afraid that you would immediately start investigating what was happening. And to be honest, at the time, I still thought you were involved. There's no way a person with your professional experience could miss these things. Eleonora assured me that you knew nothing, and for your safety and ours, we decided to temporarily leave things as they are.'

'Temporarily? You have been hiding for over two years, Sully!'

'I know,' he said and took his head in his hands. 'I want this to end, Cassy. I want to go back to my family and live a normal life.'

'You still love her, don't you?' Cassy whispered.

'Yes, and that's the problem,' he admitted.

'When did you find out they were using the warehouses for human trafficking?' she asked.

'Two years ago, but they don't use them just for that.'

'What else?'

Sully had opened his mouth to answer when a soft alarm sound came from one of the devices left on the table next to him. He motioned for her to stand and showed her a bookshelf on the wall behind her.

'This is a hidden door; pull the shelf and go through it. I'll check who it is and then follow you.'

Cassy nodded and quickly moved the shelf away. Sully was looking at one of the monitors in front of him at the time, then motioned for her to hide. He himself also headed for the makeshift door. Cassy walked forward in the dark, and after a few steps, she felt a wooden door. Sully moved her slightly aside and opened the door quietly. They ended up somewhere in the forest. She wanted to ask him where they were, but he pressed a hand over her mouth, then shook his head. The two of them sat like that for a while, listening for noise around them. Cassy had just decided that whoever it was must have walked away when two men appeared on either side of them, their stances and looks suggesting they were up to no good.

'Run!' Sully shouted and pushed her behind him. She didn't hesitate, but began to descend, hoping to find herself on the Mountain Path. Behind her, she could hear someone running, but she didn't turn to see who it was because she knew that would slow her down. She, too, was stumbling until she saw the low stone wall of the path, jumped off it, and started running as fast as she could towards the office. When she crossed the bridge and found herself on the other side of the river, she turned to see if anyone was still chasing her, but there was no one on the bridge. Whoever he was had given up chasing her. Cassy stopped for a moment to rest, then with fear in her heart for Sully, she ran again until she reached the office. Aldan saw her first, walked over and caught her before she fell to the ground. He gave her a gentle hug and helped her into the chair Burke handed him.

'What's happening?' asked RAN, who had appeared from the other room.

'Sully,' Cassy managed to say. She was still short of breath.

'Is Sully trying to kill you?'

'No,' Cassy was shaking her head. She tried to catch her breath and explain what was happening, but she couldn't. Her breathing was fast, and she just didn't have the energy to speak.

'Calm down,' said Aldan, then went to the kitchen and handed her a glass of water. She took the glass, but her hands were still shaking, and some of the water spilled onto the floor. Aldan took her hand, took the glass from her, then stood behind her and began to lightly massage her shoulders. This made her relax.

'Thank you,' she said. Then, finally able to catch her breath, she quickly told them what had happened.

'How many people were there?' RAN asked her.

'I saw two, but there may have been more.'

'What happened to Sully?'

'I do not know. I hope he managed to escape.'

'Burke and I will take two more people and go look around.'

'Can you describe where the bungalow is?' Burke asked as Aldan called for backup. Cassy described, to the best of her knowledge, where Sully had been hiding. She hoped he had managed to escape. Then she remembered that her sister-in-law might be in danger now, too.

'You must also find Eleonora and the twins,' she told RAN.

'I already sent someone to look for them,' he reassured her.

Of course, she said to herself, *he always thought two steps ahead*. He was not like her, useless and blinded by the dream of a good and peaceful life.

RAN called Zlotov and ordered him to stay with Cassy, then left the office.

'Big mess, boss,' said the young man and looked sympathetically at her. She nodded. She had just decided that she had found out what was going on in the town, and someone had interrupted them. Sully didn't have time to tell her. *But who knew where they would meet?* she wondered. Surely, no one had followed them. The two attackers came much later. Someone had told them where they were, but who? According to her, only one person knew where Sully was hiding, and that was Eleonora. *Was she really worried about her family, or was she involved in what was going on in town?* Cassy began to wonder, and the suspicion that Eleonora was behind it all began to grow with each subsequent thought. She absolutely needed to talk to her sister-in-law, she thought, but first, she needed to rest.

Cassy got up and walked into the kitchen. She made coffee for herself and Zlotov, then opened her laptop, and looked again at the people in the crowd. She had only seen one of the attackers very briefly, but she was sure she had seen him before. Cassy first looked at the photos, then watched Burke's recording several times. Finally, she saw what she was looking for. The man who chased her in the forest had stood well off to the side, and unlike everyone else, he wasn't looking at the warehouse door or the uniformed men in front of it. His gaze followed Sully, watching his every move. Perhaps he had realized that he had signalled her and then followed her. No, he hadn't followed her; Cassy was sure of that. He had barely managed to track down Sully either. Someone had told him where they were; nothing else was relevant.

Zlotov's quiet cough interrupted her thoughts.

'I have to tell you something important, boss, but I want you to promise me not to share this with others.'

Cassy looked at him, saw that he was worried, and nodded in agreement.

'Do you promise?' he asked.

'I promise, I won't tell anyone anything. I swear,' she assured him.

'Good. Six months ago, I had a date with Maggie. We were supposed to meet at her place at six o'clock in the evening, but when I got there, she was gone. I was very worried because I kept trying to call her and talk to her, but her phone kept going to voicemail. So, I decided to stay at her house and wait for her in case they kept her in the hospital. You know, it happens sometimes. Anyway, Maggie came home two hours later, shaking with fear and her clothes soaked with blood. When I asked her what happened, she told me that she had been helping with an accident and that what she saw there shocked her.'

'You checked about the crash, didn't you?' Cassy interrupted him.

'Yes, and there was none. Then I wondered why she had lied to me, but I never questioned her again. She never mentioned anything about what happened. Last night, however, she told me.' Zlotov fell silent and looked at Cassy. 'There was an accident, but it was not registered. A big lorry has crashed not far from Balkan on one of the dirt roads. The driver and the people in the lorry were injured, and Doctor Fisher and Maggie were forced to go and give them medical help.'

'Who forced them?' Cassy asked.

'I don't know, boss. But according to Maggie, Doctor Fisher knows.'

A gasp of surprise escaped Cassy's mouth. She had sensed that Fisher knew something and had decided to question him but never did. *You're a fool, Cassy, a big fool*, she scolded. But could she be to blame? She tried to justify herself and her actions. Everything was happening so fast, and it was as if thousands of knives were attacking her from a thousand directions. She didn't even have time to eat well. Cassy leaned back in the chair and folded her hands in front of her like some suspects did to protect themselves.

'I will talk to Doctor Fisher,' she promised Zlotov. First, she had to rest. Her fatigue prevented her from concentrating and doing her job well. The ringing of her phone snapped her out of her thoughts.

'We can't find Sully and Eleonora. Their kids aren't in school,' Aldan told her.

Cassy felt her mouth go dry. Everything just got worse, she told herself.

'We found a lot of documents in Sully's bungalow. Including the missing architectural plans from the Archive Warehouse,' Burke told her after he and the others returned to the office. He showed her the documents, and he and Aldan retired to the other room to look at them. Sam had retreated to the lodge with his dog, RAN had told her, and now it was just the three of them and Zlotov, who was still not fully allowed into their investigation.

Cassy stared at the papers in front of her. A number of them were marked with various marks, and Burke, after examining them more closely, separated them. Cassy stared at Sully's handwriting. It was familiar to her from somewhere else. Then she remembered the card left for her at the hospital. It was the same handwriting.

'Sully set fire to the city,' she said.

Burke nodded in agreement.

'But why would he do that?' Aldan asked.

'To stop them,' Cassy and Burke answered almost simultaneously.

'Two years is a long time for a man to hide in the forest. He had to act and do something that would allow him to return to his family,' explained the fireman. 'If it were me, I would do the same.'

'You suspected him from the very beginning, didn't you?' Cassy asked.

'Yes. Only he could make such a big fire, with only material damage. I read his file and talked to his colleagues. No one else would be able to do this, but I wondered why. Why would he risk human life? Now everything is clear to me.'

'Right?' Cassy asked. 'I, on the other hand, seem to be even more confused.'

'Think, Cassy. He did not threaten human lives; on the contrary, he saved them. Do you remember that in one of the reports it was written that, in addition to fleeing residents of the city, there were also many tourists who did not know the language? I think Sully knew there were people in the warehouses and opened the door for them.'

'No,' Cassy disagreed. 'In my opinion, the premises were empty at the time of the fire.'

'I think so too,' agreed Aldan. 'They could barely walk. They would be obvious to everyone if they were on the streets in the town. If Sully was the arsonist, then he knew what the warehouses were being used for and tried to stop them from using them again. He then searched for information on the other warehouses, by searching Leslie's house and taking the plans from the Archive Warehouse.'

'Maybe you're right,' Burke said, continuing to look at the documents.

RAN also joined them. They told him what they had found.

'It would have been easiest if Sully had come to us,' he said after listening to them.

'For some reason, he didn't want to come to us. I think he's worried about Eleonora and the kids. Someone is threatening them, RAN. Sully was convinced that someone would hurt his family if he made the wrong move.'

'Then we'd better find him as quickly as possible. And Eleonora, too. I called a few more people to help us while Cassy and Aldan rest.'

'I don't need a break,' protested Aldan.

'Don't argue with me. You and Cassy are going to Burke's house, and you're going to stay there until I call you. Take your laptops with you just in case.'

Cassy agreed.

'I will first go to get a few things from Marina's house.'

'Whatever you do, I want Aldan to be with you,' ordered RAN and then turned his back on them.

Cassy and Aldan grabbed their phones and laptops and left the office. Then, they slowly made their way to Marina's house. As they walked, Cassy continued to feel that someone was watching her. She tapped Aldan on the shoulder and gestured for him to look around. She was shivering, and that was never a good sign. When they entered Marina's house, the old woman invited them into the kitchen and did not let them go until they had eaten the lunch she had made. Then Cassy packed up and went with Aldan to Burke's house.

The house was not small, and Cassy was surprised that it had been given to Burke's family as a temporary residence after the fire. It was bigger than her sister-in-law's house, with four bedrooms and two large terraces. At the back of the house, to her surprise, there was a large garden, with a built-in barbecue shed. The shed had a corner with a bookshelf containing many books. *A great place to relax in the afternoon and make dinner,* she thought. It created a cozy family atmosphere. Children's drawings and toys, probably by Burke's daughters, were still visible in part of the living room. Cassy had dreamed of such a house. For a big family and a man to support her. She had found the man in Ron, but he was gone. One thing was certain, she had married Steve without actually being in love, and although they had tried to make the flat, they lived in a cosy, it had never worked. There was no way it could be done when the main ingredient – love – was missing. Cassy had a favourite song that she had been listening to for years, and somehow the song got stuck in her head and the lyrics perfectly matched her thoughts: '*One day your heart will find out you've been lying to it,*' was sung in the song. She had not only lied to her heart, but she had also hidden her feelings from everyone. She didn't love Steve and never had. Their relationship was fake; she had used it, hoping to start flames that were actually in a fireplace with a fake fire, the kind you put on the monitor to keep warm when you're cold.

The effect of that fire had been short-lived, as had her marriage. It was better that they didn't have children, Cassy thought, and wondered if she would ever be able to find a man to love her the way she and Ron had loved each other.

Cassy was sitting by the barbecue, lost in thought, forgetting that Aldan was in the house too. He appeared with a towel around his waist, and a pot of coffee in his hand.

'I saw that you were thinking, and I didn't want to interrupt you,' he said and sat down next to her. Cassy reached down, took two mugs from the shelf and poured coffee for them both.

'What were you thinking about?' he asked her.

'My life.'

'Everything is going to be okay, Cassy. You'll get a divorce, we'll find the human traffickers, and you'll move on. You just need time.'

'You don't understand.' She shook her head and sipped her coffee.

'Maybe I don't understand, but maybe I do, more than you think,' he said, then entered the house and returned with two bottles of still water. 'Drink; after all this stress today, you need hydration.'

'You seem to understand everything, huh?'

'Nothing like that.' He smiled sadly at her. 'I say this from experience.'

'Have you been married?' Cassy asked, surprised by her own question.

'Yes. Twice.'

'Twice?'

'Both times briefly.'

'What went wrong?'

'The first time I was young and very much in love.' Aldan smiled at the memory. 'The truth is that I was still a kid, and the girl I married had different ideas about life than I did. She wanted a big house, lots of children, and money.'

'Every woman dreams of this.'

'That's right, but you can't get them at twenty-one. At twenty-two, I was already divorced.'

'She broke your heart,' Cassy realized.

'She did. Two months after the divorce, she married a man ten years older than her, who immediately gave her everything she dreamed of.'

'I guess it was hard for you to accept it.'

'It was difficult, yes. I left my hometown and moved to the capital. Then I joined the army. A few years later, I got married again. This time, my marriage lasted four years.'

'What went wrong?' Cassy asked, although she already guessed the answer from his look.

'When you marry someone, and you lie about loving them, sooner or later, the truth comes out. There's nowhere to hide it, especially if you don't have children.'

'That's right,' Cassy agreed.

'You don't love Steve, do you? If you loved him, you would mention him more often.'

'You and I are obviously from the same club, huh? The fake love club.'

'You could say so. Sorry about your dog. Sam and Zlotov told me that you were very attached to him.'

'Yes, I loved Charlie very much,' Cassy muttered, and she and Aldan remained silent for a while. 'Some people say that time heals, and after a while, you start living with the thought that the person or pet you loved is no longer with you. But I couldn't get used to it. Ron seems to still be around me, and I would say that, as strange as it sounds, I feel Charlie now too.'

'Maybe you haven't found the man to replace Ron with yet,' suggested Aldan, and he looked into her eyes.

'And maybe I don't want to replace him. I guess that's why I stayed with Steve so long. I ran away from anyone who looked even remotely like Ron. I didn't want to lose him or replace him; I wanted him to be with me forever.'

Cassy was silent; Aldan didn't say anything either. They stayed like that, sipping their coffee, each lost in thought.

Later, Cassy took a shower and then joined Aldan in the living room. Neither of them wanted to watch a movie or listen to music. She lay down on one of the sofas and thought that she had not been in such a quiet room for a long time. The silence was overwhelming. She couldn't even hear Aldan's breathing. It was as if the surrounding walls absorbed every sound and hid it from them. It wasn't long before Cassy drifted to sleep.

When she woke up, it was dark outside. She looked up to see if Aldan was awake and saw from the reflection of the garden lamp that his eyes were open. He was awake, watching her, but saying nothing. Cassy thought again about the strange silence in the house, then closed her eyes and, for the first time in years, imagined someone hugging her. *It's all the fault of the silence,* she told herself, and then she drifted off again.

-Chapter Fourteen-

A Whirlwind

In the morning, Cassy woke up to a muffled sound and the smell of freshly brewed coffee. She looked up to see Burke and Aldan talking in the garden, then got up and joined them. Burke looked terribly tired. There were blue circles under his eyes, and his skin was pale.

'Good morning,' she greeted them. 'Where's the coffee?'

'Right here,' answered Aldan. While handing her the pot of coffee, he studied her face. 'You look better today.'

'And I feel better. I can go back to work.'

'I don't think RAN will agree with you. He ordered that you and Aldan take a break today. He also said to pass on to you that he sent you a few emails.'

'Okay, I'll look at them now.'

'Don't hurry.' Aldan stopped her. 'First, have breakfast and drink your coffee.'

Only then did Cassy notice the sandwiches he had placed in front of her.

'Marina sent them,' said Burke.

'Yeah, I'm her stepdaughter,' Cassy muttered.

'What?'

'Nothing. I'll have breakfast and go back to work. I don't care what RAN thinks; I can't stay in this house all day. The silence here is driving me crazy.'

'Okay, okay,' said Burke, raising his hands. 'Relax.'

'Sorry,' Cassy said, pulling the cup of coffee and the sandwiches towards her, and began to eat under the watchful eyes of the two men.

'Did you discover anything new?' she asked Burke.

'Yes. We found Eleonora and the children.'

Cassy breathed a sigh of relief. The last thing she wanted was more missing people.

'Did she say anything?'

'No. She is silent and insists that if we want to question her, it will be in the presence of a lawyer. We have nothing against her, Cassy. She explained that she took the children to get out of town for a while because they needed a break.'

'What mayor leaves town in a case like this? I don't believe her,' said Aldan.

'Nor do I,' Cassy said. 'Do you think she'll want to talk to me?'

'She may want to, but since there was no reason for us to keep her, shortly after RAN questioned her, we let her go. The truth is, we have nothing against her,' said Burke.

'We have nothing against anyone,' Cassy emphasized and stood up, but Burke stopped her.

'We have enough against Steve, and you know it.'

'I know, but we'll have to find him first, right? And did you manage to question the lawyer?'

'We have nothing against her either. We need something solid or someone who can tell us something more specific.'

'I might have something,' she said, and with that, she caught the attention of the two men. 'When I was in the hospital, I talked to Doctor Fisher. He didn't tell me anything specific at the time, he just mentioned, and I'll paraphrase, "In this town, nothing seems to happen, but it's like cockroaches, you think they're gone until you turn on the light and see them crawling everywhere." I thought about questioning Fisher, but I never had the time. I'd like to do it myself, though, because I already know how to approach him.'

'Okay,' agreed Burke, 'but you will have to discuss it with RAN. According to him, you missed a lot of things that happened in the town while you were the police chief.'

Aldan intervened and tried to protect Cassy. 'I think that if I had been there, I wouldn't have noticed them. Just think, almost everyone was related to Cassy and knew how to keep their secrets from her. They literally knew her every next step, and she would have had no way of suspecting anything was going on unless she happened upon it.'

'Sully found out something wrong had happened in the town,' countered Burke.

'But as far as I understood, he also found it out by accident. He only found out after two years. He was here when the former police chief was removed, and he didn't suspect anything. In my opinion, the people we are dealing with are either very smart or very scared,' said Aldan.

'I admit that I let my guard down. The town looked like any other country town. If I had looked for trouble, I would surely have found it. Although Sully's disappearance and Eleonora and Steve's reaction to his disappearance had already raised quite a few questions,' Cassy said. RAN was right; she hadn't done her job, and it would haunt her for the rest of her life. All these people tied to a wire could have been free years ago. 'We can't change the past,' she said quietly and went to take a shower. She needed to freshen up and think straight.

When she returned to the living room, Burke was already asleep in her spot on the sofa, snoring lightly.

'Apparently, this will be our common bedroom,' she said. The presence of men in the room she slept in had not bothered her for a long time; she was used to it from her work for the Intelligence Agency. What she wasn't used to was Aldan's presence. He managed to throw her off balance. He kind of reminded her of Ron, and it bothered her. Cassy wondered how to deal with the feelings she had for him. It was unexpected for her to be bothered by the nudity of a man. There was a cure for that, and it was called work. If she were working, she wouldn't be thinking about Aldan. She would get tired and fall fast asleep like last night. With that in mind, she poured herself another cup of coffee, picked up her laptop, and sat down at the table next to Aldan. He had opened his laptop too, and when he saw her sit down, he smiled at her.

'You look better,' he said.

She didn't answer him. Instead, she opened the first email from RAN and started reading. RAN's emails were always short, so when Cassy opened the first one, she was surprised by its length. In it, he gave her detailed information about Sam and Marta's marriage. The two had met at work; RAN did not specify what work. They had spent five years together, marrying at the end of the third year, shortly before the birth of their second child. RAN did not know the reason for their separation; the only thing he knew for sure was that Sam had not kept in touch with his family, although he often sought information about his children. RAN advised Cassy and Aldan to go to the lodge, and at an appropriate time, Cassy was to talk to Sam and ask him the "right" questions. Apparently, RAN knew the answers, but he didn't want to tell her.

The second email contained information about Steve. Cassy wasn't surprised by what was written in the email because she already knew all the information in the file that RAN had sent her. She also knew that there were three blank years in Steve's life. During that time, he had neither paid nor been paid. It was as if he had gone far away and returned at the end of the third year. This had worried RAN from the moment she had told him who she was going to marry. He had advised her to wait and not hurry into marrying Steve. He had also hinted to her that she was not ready for such a relationship, but Cassy had not listened to RAN. What had Steve been doing those three years? She stared at the laptop monitor and felt lost. It was like everything was going round and round. She had been trying to solve the mystery for a month and a half now – she was tired of looking over her shoulder and wondering who she could trust and who she couldn't. Cassy let out a sigh of despair, and Aldan looked up from his laptop.

'What's wrong?' he asked, looking at her again with the same look Ron had once given her. She sighed again, though for a different reason this time. 'RAN recommends that you and I go to Sam's lodge,' she said.

'And that's what this drama is about. You don't want to go there or ...?'

'No, the reason is different, but I prefer not to talk about it now. I'll go pack my stuff,' she said. She thought that within the last two months, she had moved as many times as she had ever done in her entire life. Then she remembered that she didn't have many belongings anyway. The memory of the burned flat and the things she had left there made her sad. She returned to Aldan and asked him if he minded if they went downtown first.

'Why do you want to go there? What is there?' he asked her.

She answered, 'Just memories, nothing else.'

Aldan nodded and, in turn, went to pack. As they stepped out onto the street, Cassy again felt those shivers that came when she felt someone watching her. She wondered whether to tell Aldan, but decided against it. She preferred not to bother him more than necessary. He had become so accustomed to his role as her guardian angel that he had even taken to carrying her bag. She had never let anyone do that before. *And why did she let him?* she asked herself. If she told him she felt like they were being followed, Aldan would make her come back to Burke's house, and she didn't want that.

They went to the office, talked briefly with RAN and two of their colleagues, then got a car, and Aldan drove it to the burned building where Cassy had lived until recently. To her surprise, the block was still holding. Only a few of the apartments seemed to be damaged, but the others still looked good. She got out of the car and walked into the burned entrance. All this reminded her of the fire, and she hesitated before the steps. Then she slowly began to climb them, stepping on the ashes and soot that were still around. She could hear Aldan's footsteps behind her, and his presence calmed her again. *That feeling she'd had before when Ron was around,* she thought.

When she went up to the floor where her flat was, she noticed that the front door was still open as she had left it. There were signs of fire in the hallway of the apartment, but none in the living room or kitchen. When she looked more closely, Cassy saw that someone had rummaged through their belongings, and she wondered whether they had been looking for something in particular or whether thieves were rummaging for some valuables. To her surprise, the rings Ron had given her were still in the jewellery box. As well as her other valuables. She opened a bag and started putting a few of Charlie's toys inside, along with one of the leashes she used to take him for walks.

'People will think I'm crazy,' she said to herself, forgetting that Aldan was also with her in the flat.

'It's normal to want to take something as a keepsake. People do it all the time.' He tried to calm her down. She ignored him. She wanted to be alone here with her belongings, but she knew Aldan wouldn't agree to leave her alone in the dilapidated building. It would be useless to argue with him.

When she had collected everything she wanted to take, Cassy took one last look around the rooms, and without saying anything, she walked past Aldan and out the front door. He followed her almost immediately.

The two travelled in silence on the way to Sam's lodge. Cassy had her laptop open and was studying Doctor Fisher. *What did he know?* she wondered. She had to call him and convince him to meet her. Her instinct told her that he would not agree easily. Sure, she could call him into the office for questioning, but Cassy thought that if they talked informally and she got Fisher to relax, it would be easier for her to get information out of him.

They had almost reached the lodge when she got an email from her lawyer. Steve had signed the divorce papers. This surprised her so much that she pulled the laptop closer to her eyes and read the email twice more. She hadn't expected Steve to agree to a divorce so quickly.

'What's wrong?' Aldan asked, noticing her confusion. She blinked twice, then closed the laptop and made herself more comfortable in the seat. Since she didn't answer right away, Aldan looked at her intently.

'Steve signed the divorce papers,' she said, and felt her mouth begin to dry. Why did this news shock her, she wondered. That was exactly what she wanted, wasn't it?

'So, you're divorced now?' Aldan asked.

'Not yet, but the lawyer thinks that if one of us doesn't make any new claims on property or whatever, the divorce decree will be out in two weeks.'

'You don't seem happy about the news,' he said, and again gave her that look that took her breath away.

'On the contrary, I am satisfied. I'm just surprised it happened so quickly.'

'Forward me the email. I want to know who his lawyer is who helped him with the divorce papers. Maybe we'll find Steve through him.'

'Of course,' Cassy said. This possibility never crossed her mind. Again, she wasn't thinking professionally, she chided herself. RAN was right; she wasn't ready to go back to work at all. The feelings she felt were like being in a whirlwind. Everything was flying around her, and it was hard for her to catch anything or hold on to anything and feel a solid footing. She was blinded as if by a strong wind accompanied by rain and snow. *I have to do something*, she told herself. *I have to stop and calm down; only then will I see what is happening around me.* Cassy closed the laptop and stared at the beautiful forest they were driving through. A few minutes later, they arrived at the turnoff to the lodge, and Buggy, Sam's dog, came to meet them. Cassy stroked his head, and the dog's eyes seemed to ask her a question, *Where's Charlie?*

'Charlie's gone, Buggy,' Cassy said, and tears fell from her eyes. She knelt down, hugged the dog, and began to cry openly. Sam and Aldan were watching her, but neither of them interrupted her, and the dog, seeming to understand her distress, sat still, resting his head on her shoulder.

When her tears subsided, Cassy stood up, greeted Sam, and walked slowly into the lodge.

'I'm not sure that this is the place where I can rest,' she told Aldan. 'Too many memories.'

'I agree. We will look for something else,' he promised and dialled RAN's phone.

Cassy looked around. Sam had gone into the kitchen and was making tea.

'I won't ask if there's anything new about the case because I know you can't tell me,' he said and handed her a cup of her favourite tea.

'I can't tell you because I'm also suspended for a few days. I came here because I have a few questions about your marriage to Marta. RAN said that if I ask you, you will tell me in detail why you broke up.'

'Is that what he said?' Sam was surprised.

'Yes. Do you want to talk about it?'

Sam turned his back on her for a moment, then he motioned her to the porch door. She went outside and sat on one of the chairs there.

'RAN ... did he tell you how Marta and I met?' he asked.

'No, he just mentioned that it was during work.'

'Okay. Wait here for a moment. I'll tell you, but I wouldn't want Aldan to overhear.'

Sam re-entered the lodge. She heard him talking to Aldan. He then returned to her.

'Don't you believe him?'

'I trust only you,' Sam said and looked at her intently, kind of going to tell her what she wanted to know, but she didn't have to share it with anyone.

She saw Aldan leave the house and retire to one of the gazebos on the lawn. From there, he could watch them, but he couldn't hear what they were talking about. Cassy could see the sparkle in his blue eyes. His chestnut hair was now dishevelled. He seemed to be staring at her. *He is still getting used to being a bodyguard*, Cassy thought, and somehow that calmed her instead of angering her.

Sam also watched Aldan for a while, then sipped his tea and looked Cassy in the eye.

'What I'm going to tell you will probably shock you, but I want you to promise me that you won't comment on it to anyone.'

Cassy blinked twice. Surprises had become her specialty; one more or less didn't matter anymore.

'I promise not to tell anyone,' she assured him and waited to hear what he would tell her.

'It is true that Marta and I met at work. I worked undercover as a bartender in a strip club in a small town near Rila, and Marta was a stripper.'

Sam waited to see how Cassy would take the news, but she wasn't as shocked as he probably expected. Two of her friends paid for college by working in strip clubs.

'What were you investigating then?' she asked him.

'Human trafficking,' he answered, and only now did she understand why he expected her to be shocked.

'Was Marta one of them? Trafficked?' Cassy asked.

'Yes. Her real name was Larisa Nikolaevna. After we uncovered the trafficking scheme, I helped her change her name, and I married her.'

'You took a big risk.'

'That's right, but I have to admit that for most of the time we were a family, the risk was worth it. She was the most beautiful woman I have ever met. Smart and beautiful – a dangerous combination, if you ask me.'

'Why did you split?'

'Because of my work. I had taken on a case involving a woman. It's not pleasant to tell you, but so that you understand what happened then and so that you don't ask yourself any more questions, I'll try to explain it. The woman I was investigating was, for some reason, attracted to me. She found me very sexy.' Sam smiled at the memory. 'I somehow succumbed to the feeling that she adored me. After a while, I got carried away. Although my closeness to this woman helped me to get the job done, I then put her in jail. I'm not making excuses; I'm just saying that these were the consequences.'

'Marta found out, did she?'

'Yes, you got it. I still don't know how she found out; someone must have told her. The moment I got home, I found my things packed. Two days later, Marta called me and told me that she had filed for divorce and expected me to cause no problems for her, and to agree quickly. One of her conditions was that I would not contact the children without her permission.'

'And you agreed?' Cassy was surprised.

'Of course, I didn't agree, but in the end, she won. She had found pictures of the woman and me in question somewhere and promised to give them as evidence in court if I didn't sign the agreement. It would have ruined not only my marriage but also my career. I finally signed.'

'Do you regret it now?' Cassy asked.

'Of course, I regret it. Every time I wanted to see my children; she found an excuse not to let me see them. Although Marta and I were divorced, we kept in touch. I've talked to her more often than any other woman over the years. I knew every detail of what was going on in my children's lives, but I couldn't see them. For some reason, she wouldn't let me meet them for years. When I finally did, they no longer remembered me. To them, I was a close friend of their mother. After this meeting, I went into shock and, for a while, into a deep depression. Do you know how it feels to talk to your own children, know everything about them, and to have them treat you like a stranger? It's a terrible feeling, and I hope you never experience it, Cassy.'

'That's why you came here. You told me that you wanted to get closer, but you couldn't.'

'I didn't make it, but here I could at least talk to them and see my grandchildren from time to time.'

'But why didn't you tell Eleonora and Steve who you were?'

'I was waiting for the right moment, which never came.'

'Eleonora is still here. You can talk to her.'

'She has enough headaches now – a father coming out of nowhere will not be good news.'

'If I were you, I would try. You have nothing to lose by telling her.'

'Probably, but I might lose her forever this way.'

Cassy told herself he was right. No one knew how Eleonora would react to this news. Maybe she wouldn't be too happy about Sam.

'Thank you for telling me,' she said and patted him on the shoulder in a friendly way.

'Cassy, no one knows who Marta really is, even RAN. He only knows part of the story. Let's leave it that way. Her past won't change anything.'

'I won't tell anyone,' she promised. Then she looked at the beautiful view in front of her. *And I thought my life was complicated*, she thought.

'Steve and I are getting a divorce,' she said after a short silence. 'I guess we should have done it a long time ago, but probably neither of us wanted to take the initiative.'

'I know he is my son, Cassy, but it was clear to everyone that he was not for you. You need someone who understands you and supports you.'

Someone like Aldan, she thought, looking up at him. What the hell was wrong with her? She didn't know him well. She looked over at Sam and realized he was looking at Aldan as well.

'Yes, you need someone like him,' Sam said to her surprise. 'Someone who will understand the importance of your work and who will give you support. Take my advice, Cassy, and don't marry anyone outside the business again. Nothing good will come of it.'

With that, Sam left the porch, and she realized what he had just told her. She had not known if her infatuation with Aldan was obvious or if Sam had just been giving him as an example. Her stormy feelings intensified, and Cassy felt that she was no longer in control of them. Fury, anger, and passion – all swirling into one. She needed to calm down, she kept telling herself, but calm never came.

-Chapter Fifteen-

Lost

Cassy had taken Buggy and gone for a walk in the woods, hoping to collect her thoughts. The dog walked by her side and nudged her leg from time to time as if to ask if she was okay.

'I'm fine,' she said and continued walking. Then she started running. And as she ran, she cried; she didn't know why. Then she got tired and sweaty, and the shivers that she felt after a workout went through her body. Perhaps cleansing her soul and body. She stopped and looked around to see where she was, then looked at Buggy.

'I guess we got lost, huh?' She smiled, fully aware that the dog knew very well where he was. 'Let's go back,' she said, and Buggy started forward with a bark. It turned out they were not far from the lodge. As they approached, Cassy saw Sam and Aldan arguing. They obviously hadn't seen her approach.

'Leave her alone,' said Aldan. Sam was about to say something, but then Buggy slipped between his legs, almost knocking him over. Aldan turned and, upon seeing her, smiled at her.

'So, you came back,' he said. 'I thought you ran away.'

'I might do it someday,' she said and quickly entered the lodge. She wanted to shower, eat, and go to sleep as quickly as possible. Aldan and Sam followed her, and the lodge host called after her that dinner would be ready in half an hour. It reminded her that she hadn't eaten in almost an entire day. She had made it a habit not to eat well. *I don't need food,* Cassy thought, *I need peace.*

After showering, Cassy joined the two men in the kitchen and ate the chicken fillet Sam had prepared for her. She stood to go back to her room, but Aldan grabbed her arm and stopped her.

'We need to talk,' he said, and without letting go of her hand, he led her outside. The sun had already set, but it was still light on the porch. When they were outside, Cassy pulled her hand from his and crossed her arms over her chest. He looked at her, and she saw a glint in his eyes.

'Are you afraid of me, Cassy?' he asked her, relaxing his body on one of the chairs in front of her.

'No.'

'Then why do you cross your arms like that every time you talk to me? You know what body language says about such a gesture.'

'I know. I just feel uncomfortable around you,' she admitted and immediately regretted what she had said.

'Uncomfortable?' He smiled.

'Yes. You act like you're my bodyguard, and you look at me like you understand everything.'

'Maybe I understand.'

'You do not know me.'

'Nor you me,' he countered.

Cassy was silent. She felt even more confused than before.

'Come, let's go for a walk,' she suggested after a short, painful silence. He got up, and they both headed for the gazebo where he had been working until recently.

'Do you have any new information?' she asked, diverting the subject in another direction.

'Actually, yes. Steve hired a lawyer online and sent a power of attorney authorizing the lawyer to make decisions for him. They haven't met in person, so we don't have a lead on him yet. The power of attorney was issued on the day you filed for divorce. In fact, RAN was surprised you didn't tell him.'

'I only mentioned it to you because I didn't expect the events to develop so quickly.'

'If you divorce and we find more of his buildings, we won't be able to enter without a warrant,' Aldan said as he watched her quizzically. Cassy looked away from him.

'No one should be angry about me wanting to divorce a criminal as quickly as possible. RAN should be happy about my divorce, not worried about it.'

'If you ask me, you did the right thing, and you don't owe an explanation to anyone why and when you decided to divorce.'

'I'm not asking you. I haven't asked him either,' she answered and started to get up. However, he took her hand and forced her to stay.

'There's one more thing. Your dog, Charlie, was shot with the weapon that was used in two other murders.'

Cassy blinked. For the past few hours, she'd been trying to forget what Charlie had looked like before she buried him. Now the picture appeared before her eyes again.

'I'm sorry, I know it's hard for you, but I thought it was better for you to know.'

'Thank you. Where did the murders take place?'

'Perhaps it is better to tell you first *when* they took place. Thirty years ago.'

'Thirty years ago?' Cassy asked with surprise.

'Yes. In a town near Rila.'

'What is the name of the town?'

'Sakar,' answered Aldan and looked at her again with that concerned look that made her legs shake. 'Both murders appear to be executions. A woman and a man, in different parts of the town. Burke and Zlotov will send us details about the murders.'

'Strange that someone uses the same weapon after so many years, don't you think?' she asked.

'Yes. My guess is that whoever did it was unprepared and used whatever weapon was at hand. He was in a hurry to move out, otherwise he wouldn't have left so many traces and evidence.'

'I guess you're right.'

'We're going to find out who killed your dog, Cassy. I promise I won't stop searching until I find out.'

'Don't talk to me like a defenceless woman, Aldan, because I'm not like that. I need a day or two off work, nothing more. Then I can find whoever killed Charlie and blew up the town on my own.'

'Sully blew up the town, and you know it.'

'Someone forced Sully to do it. This is the person I will look for.' Cassy raised her voice, and this forced Aldan to take her hand.

'Calm down,' he said quietly, and pulled her to him. She tried to pull away, but he wouldn't let her go. Instead, he held her head with his free hand and turned it so she could see his eyes. Then he leaned down slightly and kissed her. He had loosened his grip, but instead of pulling away, she pressed herself against him and kissed him back.

'The last thing I need is an affair right now,' she whispered in his ear, and she slowly pulled away from him.

'You are no longer married,' he reminded her and pulled her to him again. This time, she didn't resist but let him kiss her once more. Then she got up and went back to her room alone, though inwardly, she wanted him to follow her.

To distract herself, Cassy turned on the laptop, but before she started reading her emails, she decided to make herself some tea. Back in the room, she opened the email in which RAN informed her that if she felt better the next day, she could return to work. He had also arranged a new doctor's test to restore her driving license. She opened the second email, but a noise coming from the bathroom made her leave the room. Sam and Aldan were still on the first floor. Cassy went into the bathroom and saw that the wind had knocked a few things off the shelf near the window. She picked them up, closed the window, and went back to her room. Then she started reading the email with information about the Sakar murders. Two strip club owners had been killed. The investigation had established that they were Russians involved in human trafficking. A red light flashed in Cassy's mind. She sipped her tea and continued reading. The murders had been done in the same way, a kind of execution. Cassy's vision blurred as she read. She rubbed her eyes, assuming tiredness was the cause, but then realized she was drifting off. Shortly after, her body slumped helplessly on the bed.

-Chapter Sixteen-

Smouldering Embers

Someone was pushing her, and Cassy was trying to resist. Then she felt she couldn't move. She tried to open her eyes, but it was difficult. Cassy felt like she was in a fog, like her brain couldn't function. Then she heard a whisper, but she couldn't make out who was speaking or what they said. She tried to move again, but she couldn't. She made an effort to raise her hand, but something stopped her. Then her vision cleared a little, but she could only see silhouettes.

'Cassy, can you hear me?' She heard a familiar voice. 'Cassy, look at me. I know you can; we lowered your dose, and you should be conscious by now.'

Cassy made another attempt to open her eyes, and this time she saw Marta's face in front of her.

'Marta? Where am I?' she managed to whisper.

'We will get there soon,' the old woman told her, smiling at her. There was something ominous about her smile, Cassy thought, and she tried to rise again. When she couldn't, she looked down at her body and saw that she was bound in a straitjacket.

'What?' she asked, horrified.

'Calm down, calm down, don't be impatient. I will tell you everything.'

'Sam? Aldan?' she tried to speak, but Marta patted her head gently and asked her not to speak.

'Only I will speak today. That's the game, don't you understand?'

Cassy tried to free herself again, but Marta pressed her down hard, squeezing her chest, and Cassy couldn't catch her breath.

'That's better,' said the old woman after a while. 'I guess you're wondering where you are. You are in a hospital for, let's say, "naughty" patients like you.'

Cassy was horrified by Marta's tone and the way she was looking at her.

'My people brought you here six months ago. Yeah, it's unbelievable, isn't it? Six whole months where no one knows where you are, and almost no one is looking for you anymore. Your people don't want to waste their time looking for you. They quickly forgot you.'

'Why am I here?' Cassy asked.

'I already told you because you are naughty. Your only job was to make my son happy, but you failed. You were supposed to be a cover for our business as well, but you failed there. Not that he's any better than you. Three years in this clinic were not enough for him to learn how to control his passions. That lawyer had taken his senses away, and you were a fool who didn't notice a thing.' Marta laughed, and Cassy felt cold from her laughter.

'You see, Steve was never smart; Eleonora was smarter. True, she married Sully against my will, but now she realizes her mistake; she has learned from it. Steve, for his part, will never wise up. I think I'll leave him here until I find him another suitable wife for my work. You played your part, Cassy, although I expected more from you.'

'Why am I here?' Cassy asked. 'Why don't you just kill me?'

'Because I'm not done with you yet. When I'm done, you'll quickly find yourself where you belong.'

Marta motioned to someone next to her, and Cassy felt a slight sting in her arm.

'Now you will fall asleep again, Sleeping Beauty. I woke you up just to find out if you were still in your right mind. In a few months, you won't be thinking straight, and then I'll use what's left of you. Until then, sleep and remember my face. And don't expect help. No one knows you're here, and no one will find you.'

Cassy tried to free herself again. She heard Marta's voice.

'Don't waste your energy. I have already extinguished the fire in you; soon not a single flame will remain.'

Cassy was trying to resist the opiate she had been given. She squeezed her eyes shut and remembered the burning city and the moment she had almost lost her life. It was all Marta's fault. She might have thought she had put out the fire, but Cassy could still feel the smouldering embers inside her. One small mistake on Marta's part and that ember would turn into a raging fire. *Make one little mistake, Marta,* Cassy prayed, *just one. Then my time will come, I will set you on fire and turn you to ashes,* she promised.

Then, the opiate took over her body, and Cassy flopped helplessly onto the bed. However, the embers inside her continued to smoulder.

To be continued...

Fire

Book 2

Embers

After Cassy's disappearance, Aldan is the only one who looks for her and who works on the case. Almost everyone believes she is dead, but not him.

After his dog, Bandit, finds her, Aldan and RAN try to find out who is behind the human trafficking and her kidnapping. However, the investigation seems to be going around in circles. Someone is always one step ahead of them. Someone who knows well not only Cassy, but everyone involved in the investigation.

hrisisart@gmail.com

www.authorhristinabloomfield.com

Instagram: @hristinabloomfield

Also by Hristina Bloomfield

Deeply In the Soul

"Deeply in the Soul" (2022) - 5 stars Readers' Favorite,

Honorable Mentions at the 2023 Hollywood Book Festival,

Honorable Mentions at the Paris Book Festival 2023

Xena is forced to run away when she finds out her boyfriend sold her. After years of running, her past finally catches up with her ...

The story follows Xena who finds herself in the situation of a victim but manages to escape. After her boyfriend is unable to return a loan, she is sold to the moneylender who wants her to work for him as a prostitute. She flees her hometown and tries to start a new life, but her past keeps catching up with her. Xena struggles to find her way as each time she gets to a good place, she has to run again. After months of solitude, Xena finally trusts Agent Dobrevski who helps Xena to face her trauma in order to finally live a normal life. The story begins in a small mountain town in Eastern Europe and ends in Cornwall, UK.

Deeply in the Soul is crime fiction; however, it also includes themes such as trauma, grief, romance, action and friendship. Xena's story is not only tragic but inspirational too.

Kurt

Books's awards and stickers

"Kurt" (2023) 5 stars Golden sticker from Reader View,

Honorable Mentions at the 2023 Hollywood Book Festival

Honorable Mentions at the Paris Book Festival 2023

His music, his dog Dante, and his motorcycle were his life until one day everything changed.

Fifty-six-year-old rock star Kurt and his rock band set up to create their new album in Cornwall. They are joined by the lyricist Leah, who agrees to help them with the lyrics for the new songs. Everything is going well until one night one of the band's roadie and Leah's taxi driver are killed. Clues led to two different killers. One wants to kill Kurt and the other Leah. Then both are subsequently shot by a sniper.

The investigation was unsuccessful, and the police inspectors send Leah far away and use Kurt to get the killers to show up.

However, new revelations about Leah's identity confuse the musician. Kurt's life will turn in an unexpected direction for him, and new revelations will make Kurt realize that he has unwittingly intervened in something from which he will hardly be able to escape.

Becky

"Becky" (2022) 5 stars Readers' Favorite.

Her life will pass through your fingers as you read this book.

Sixteen-year-old Becky is raped and left lying with multiple stab wounds on the Cornwall coast. Instead of supporting and helping her in this difficult time, her parents send her to London, where her cousin Arnie promises to take care of her. Arnie and his roommates Paul and Alex help her recover. When the police fail to find the perpetrators, the three men hire private detectives to help with the investigation. Becky accepts their help and in time, she and the lawyer Alex become very good friends. The difficulties they have to go through even bring them closer together. Becky and Alex fight both against her abusers and against her family, which keeps causing her trouble. After many vicissitudes, Becky finally finds justice. But fate does not let her enjoy her new life. She experiences loss after loss.

Becky's story has pain and betrayal as well as friendship, hope, and very strong love, the loss of which will be difficult for her.

Mother

I will get my daughter back.

Thea is separated from her daughter in the first few hours after her birth. Betrayed by her family and the father of her child, she does everything possible to find her. Thea's desire to get her daughter back is so great that it surprises not only her family but also the police. An investigation revealed that her baby was one of many children sold over the years.

The traces of the adoptive parents appear and disappear, and finding her daughter turns out to be more difficult than Thea and the investigative team expected.

The power of a mother's love is at the heart of this book.

The Story of a Thief

Tony was born into a family of thieves. His life seems predestined, until his girlfriend Eva disappears suddenly. For several years he put all his skills into finding her, even working in the police, but there is no sign of his girlfriend. In several of the investigations he leads, Tony works with a psychic who uses Tarot cards. He is so impressed by her gift so he decides to tell her his story with the hope that she will help him to find Eva. However, it turns out that Isabella's life is no less complicated than his. The two have a lot in common and this creates tension and romance in their relationship. In the course of their investigation, Tony and Isabella discover that nothing is as it seems.

Printed in Dunstable, United Kingdom

81923758R00150